RICHARD HAPPER

365

REASONS
TO BE PROUD TO BE
ENGLISH

MAGICAL MOMENTS IN OUR GREAT HISTORY

PORTICO

To my English rose, Rachel.

First published in Great Britain in 2014 by

Portico Books
10 Southcombe Street
London
W14 0RA

An imprint of Anova Books Company Ltd

Copyright © Portico Books, 2014

ISBN 978 1 909396 71 5

A CIP catalogue record for this book is available
from the British Library.

10 9 8 7 6 5 4 3 2 1

Printed and bound by Bookwell, Finland

This book can be ordered direct from the publisher at
www.anovabooks.com

'*There is a forgotten, nay almost forbidden word, which means more to me than any other. That word is England.*'
Sir Winston Churchill

'*The inhabitants are extremely proud and overbearing. They care little for foreigners, but scoff and laugh at them.*'
German author describing visit to England by Frederick, Duke of Württemberg, in 1592.

INTRODUCTION

In this country we have so much to be proud of that, damn it all, old chap, it's high time we stopped being so bloody *English* about our achievements.

We should stand on top of the highest building in Europe (The Shard) and shout, in the most internationally popular language, about our accomplishments to the world. Of course, we could also write a letter about our deeds, stick a stamp (Penny Black was the world's first, in 1840) on the envelope and pop it in a pillar-box (invented by novelist William Thackeray), then broadcast a show on TV (first demonstrated in London) or indeed blog about it on the World Wide Web (invented by Englishman Tim Berners-Lee).

To give you lots of fine English things to crow about, we have scoured the history books and collected the excellent, the exceptional, the extraordinary and, of course, the eccentric achievements that will have every English reader feeling proud they are a citizen of this green and pleasant land.

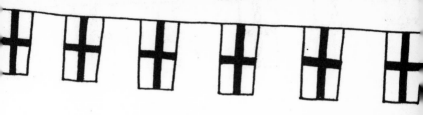

Here in these pages you will find proof that the English custom of driving on the left is right, while the right is wrong. That an Englishman wrote the American national anthem – and which English park New York's Central Park was based on. Tales of how English engineers built the roads, railways, bridges and canals that connect the modern world together. How our inventors save millions of lives all over the world, and suck dirt off carpets better than anyone else. How our explorers went where no one had gone before (but only after stocking up on champagne at Fortnum & Mason first, obviously), how our writers created a literary canon that is second to none, and how our musicians, like the Beatles, the Stones and Oasis, went rocking all over the world.

Then, and only then, will we relax with a nice cup of tea – or even a glass of our more jolly liquid invention, the gin and tonic.

So, come on – join with me now and say it loud, 'I'm English and I'm proud!'

JANUARY

CHEQUE YOUR CHANGE, MONSIEUR

1 We English have always had an insatiable urge for both overseas travel and buying alarming amounts of tourist tat while we're abroad. So it's no surprise really that the world's first ever traveller's cheques went on sale in London today in 1772. Issued by the London Credit Exchange Company, they could be used in 90 European cities. Where, no doubt, local agents eyed travellers up and down before grumpily agreeing to cash them and charging an apparently random amount of commission.

KIPLING WRITES 'IF'

'If' by Rudyard Kipling is probably the world's most stirring and frequently quoted poem. Its quiet wisdom, a reflection on the beauty of living a virtuous and humble life, adorns office walls, is spoken publically at major rallies and is displayed at countless public monuments across the land. It's even framed on the wall of the players' entrance to Centre Court at Wimbledon. It is the quintessential English poem, written by a very English poet. Kipling was inspired to write the inspirational verse after a colonial raid executed by Sir Leander Starr Jameson in Transvaal province, South Africa, which finished on this day in 1896. The raid was a bloody disaster and its failure helped incite the Second Boer War. Still, the poem is jolly nice.

THE IRON LADY'S SOFTER SIDE

When Margaret Thatcher became the longest-serving Prime Minister of the 20th century today in 1988, the event defined an era of political and social history. And while her politics might have divided the nation, we can all unite in appreciation of her *other* major contribution to English life: as a young chemist she helped perfect the soft-style ice cream dispensed in ice-cream vans – 99 out of 100 for that one, Maggie.

LONDON OFFICIALLY THE CENTRE OF THE WORLD

4 You think train timetables are tricky to read nowadays? In the early 19th century most cities in England (and throughout the world) had their own idea of what time it was. With faster trains and increased international trade this became a nightmare – a definitive world time was essential. The meridian at Greenwich Observatory was established today in 1851, and in 1884 this was accepted as the planet's prime meridian. Longitude and time zones have been aligned with London ever since. Greenwich got the nod because 72 per cent of the world's commerce depended on British sea charts – and because it annoyed the French intensely. They went into a cream puff and kept using the Paris meridian until 1914.

WILLIAM SMITH'S GEM OF AN IDEA

5 On this dark winter night back in 1796, a young man supervising the construction of a canal in Somerset was sitting in a coaching inn when he had an idea that would change the shape of the world. William 'Strata' Smith realised that the Earth's geological layers could be dated by the fossils within them. Using this technique he produced the first geological map of

Britain, and the concept of mapping strata (the layers of sedimentary rock) has since become indispensable to oil, gold and diamond exploration. Smith is now affectionately referred to as the 'Father of English Geology' – which would then make Mother Nature his wife, surely?

STONES START TO ROLL

Mick, Keith and the rest of the Rolling Stones rolled out of London on their first headline UK tour today in 1964. This was the tour that broke the band on a national level, following hot on the heels of another successful English beat combo called The Beatles (or something). Originally, the Stones were deemed just another blues cover band, but their inspired songwriting (although their first Top 20 hit was, in fact, written by Lennon & McCartney) and enthralling live act helped shape the 60s London scene, before they became the most long-lived and influential English band of all time. And to think, Mick and Keef met by chance on a Dartford train in 1960.

NICE ICE, BABY

7 Before this day in 1876, if you wanted to totter about on ice skates while teenagers zoomed around you in circles trying to knock each other over, you had to go to a frozen lake. Then a clever fellow called John Gamgee opened his Glaciarium in London. He placed insulating layers of earth, cow hair and timber over which he ran copper pipes carrying a solution of glycerine, ether, nitrogen peroxide and water. This cooled the pipes. All Gamgee had to do then was put water on top and *voilà* – the world's first artificial ice rink.

THE TWO QUEENS

8 Luxury ocean liners are a proud part of English heritage that has seen a recent resurgence in popularity. The Cunard RMS *Queen Mary 2* was christened by the Queen at Southampton Docks today in 2004, and at 151,400 gross tons, 1,132 feet long and with room for 3,056 passengers, she was the largest, longest, widest, tallest and most expensive passenger ship ever built. She is still the largest ocean liner ever – there are bigger cruise ships, but they are rather vulgar, don't you think? Liners are so much more, well, *English*.

SEND IN THE CLOWNS

9 Philip Astley was a brilliant trick rider with a knack for showmanship. He set up a riding show in a field behind what is now Waterloo station in London, today in 1768, and his phenomenal horseback acrobatics soon wowed the crowds. Uniquely, Astley had his horses run in a circle. This put the action in the centre of the crowd and generated centrifugal force to give the rider stability. His ring diameter of 42 feet (13 metres) is still standard today. And it was Astley who introduced a clown in between the main events, thereby laying the foundations for both the modern circus and McDonalds' future advertising strategy.

WORLD'S FIRST UNDERGROUND

10 Next time you're strap-hanging in 100-degree heat on the Circle Line, don't despair, take pride! You are travelling on a pioneering marvel of transportation – the world's first underground railway line. The Metropolitan Railway opened today in 1863 and originally took delighted passengers only between Paddington and Farringdon. But the Tube soon expanded across London, and is still one of the biggest metros in the world, with 270 stations and 250 miles of track.

YE OLDE NATIONAL LOTTERY

11 Our national love for the lottery actually has a long history – the first was chartered by Queen Elizabeth I and drawn today in 1569. This aimed to raise money for the 'reparation of the havens and strength of the Realme, and towardes such other publique good workes'. The government deficit, in other words. The government later went on to sell lottery ticket rights to brokers, who then hired agents and runners to sell them. These brokers eventually became modern-day stockbrokers. So, next time you play the lottery and don't win, blame them.

FOR EVER, FOR EVERYONE

12 When English social reformer Octavia Hill, solicitor Robert Hunter and clergyman Hardwicke Rawnsley got together today in 1894 to form a preservation society, they could hardly have imagined how successful they would ultimately be. Now their creation, the National Trust, has saved many of England's best-loved buildings and landscapes from ruin. The Trust now owns 200 historic houses, 630,000 acres of land (nearly 1.5 per cent of the total land mass of England, Wales and Northern Ireland) and has 3.7 million members. It has also inspired dozens of similar organisations around the world.

ALL RISE FOR ROSE

13 Rose Heilbron from Liverpool helped bring England into a new age (long overdue) of sexual equality in 1972 when she became the first female judge to sit at the Old Bailey. She was a role model for women in many respects, becoming the first female King's Counsel in England and the first to lead in a murder case, today in 1950.

SLIDING INTO HISTORY

14 England doesn't have alpine weather (no matter how much the train companies bleat otherwise), but we did help create many modern winter sports. Well-to-do Victorian gents wintering in St Moritz began bolting delivery boys' sledges together and racing them down the town's ice-packed roads, so creating bobsleighing (or tobogganing, if you prefer). And today in 1885 the famous, or should I say notorious, Cresta Run was opened. The track is 1,212m (3,978ft) of ice and is one of the few bobsleighing tracks dedicated to skeleton sledging. It is owned and operated by the male-only 'Cresta Club', whose daring members are largely still English gentlemen.

THE NEW MUSEUM

When a museum opened in an old house on London's Great Russell Street today in 1759 it **15** didn't exactly set the world on fire. It housed a couple of dusty library collections and the antiquities of noted physician Sir Hans Sloane (who also gave his name to Sloane Square). But the idea of the museum was something utterly new and powerful: it would be owned by the nation, free to all, and would collect *everything*. It now has more than seven million objects and artefacts, making the British Museum one of the most comprehensive records of human culture in the world. Incidentally, the first house considered for the museum, Buckingham Palace, was rejected for its unsuitable location.

TOP HAT AND TALES

The story goes that, today in 1797, a haberdasher called John Hetherington was **16** arraigned before the Lord Mayor of London on a charge of breach of the peace and inciting a riot. His crime? Venturing out in public wearing the first top hat. Officers stated that 'several women fainted at the unusual sight, while children screamed and dogs yelped'. Stella McCartney would kill for that sort of publicity.

HOW'S THAT?

17 Cricket may have its slow moments (unless the Barmy Army launches a conga, of course), but that just makes it one of the few sports where you can go and queue at the bar for twenty minutes and not really miss much, which is obviously a good thing. Now the world's favourite bat-and-ball game (it has a much more international appeal than baseball), its history stretches way back to Tudor England, with the first mention of the sport recorded on this day in 1598, referred to as 'creckett', and in a court case, no less.

GREAT SCOTT

18 We English love the plucky underdog, and no one personifies that more than Robert Falcon Scott from Plymouth. Better known as Captain Scott, he was fiercely determined, brave, headstrong and ultimately eloquent in the face of death, even if he is best known for being a total failure. He became a great English hero for getting to the South Pole just *one* month after Roald Amundsen. He discovered his rival's tent at the bottom of the world and turned for home, dejected but noble, today in 1912. After two more months slogging across the snow in savage conditions, his team perished within 11 miles of safety. Jolly good effort, Scott, old man!

BELLS FOR HEAVEN AND HELL

Loughborough has been an internationally famous bell-making town since the mid-14th century. The firm of John Taylor & Co opened their foundry here today in 1839, and this is still the largest bell foundry in the world. Among its many famous church bells are 'Great Paul' of St Paul's Cathedral, at 37,483lb (17 tons) the largest bell ever cast in Britain. They also made rock band AC/DC's 2,000lb bronze 'Hell's Bell', used on their *Back in Black* tour in 1980. This bell is pitched to the note 'A'.

I CALL THIS HOUSE TO ORDER

20 Simon de Montfort was a nobleman who rebelled against Henry III and became, briefly, acting ruler of England. He called on elected representatives from every county in England to meet at Kenilworth, which they did today in 1265. Although it was dissolved within a month, and de Montfort would be killed at the Battle of Evesham later that year, this created the first directly elected parliament in medieval Europe and made de Montfort one of the fathers of modern democracy.

BADMINTON SERVES TWO SPORTS

21 Far from being just the game you play when it's too rainy for tennis, badminton deserves respect as the fastest racquet sport in the world – the shuttle can reach 200mph (although not when I play). It grew from another ancient English game, battledore and shuttlecock, but the modern version with a net was first played at Badminton House in Gloucestershire and popularised in an article in *The Cornhill Magazine* today in 1863. That stately pile is also home to another English sporting institution, the Badminton Horse Trials. The horses jump fences rather than do anything with racquets...

AND THE CROWD GOES WILD...

Football fans the world over got a new treat today with the first ever live radio commentary on a match, between Arsenal and Sheffield United at Highbury. The year was 1927. To accompany the broadcast, the *Radio Times* published a pictorial grid of the pitch divided into eight squares to help listeners place the ball as the commentary was spoken. One theory states that the phrase 'back to square one' was coined by one of the commentators during this match.

THE WORLD'S MARKETPLACE

Today in 1571 saw the opening of the country's first specialist commercial building – the Royal Exchange in London. Queen Elizabeth I bestowed the building with its royal title and, more importantly, its licence to sell alcohol. For the best part of the next four centuries, it would be the centre of commerce in the capital, helping the City become the world's primary business centre. In the 17th century, stockbrokers were barred from the Royal Exchange because of their rude manners – a financial regulation we can all be proud of.

SCOUT AND ABOUT

24

Lord Robert Baden-Powell was a Boer War hero who was impressed by the ability of young lads to act as scouts and messengers in the war in Africa. He believed their resourcefulness and initiative could be encouraged in civilian life. On his return to England, he put his ideas into practice at a camp in Dorset and today in 1908 published a book, *Scouting for Boys*. Now more than 28 million people worldwide enjoy scouting, making it one of England's most enduring exports.

SAY 'CHEESE'

25

Frenchman Louis Daguerre is often thought of as the father of photography, but Dorset-born William Talbot is actually the daddy. Talbot had been taking photographs for five years when Daguerre exhibited his first pictures in early 1839. Talbot promptly showed his five-year-old shots at the Royal Institution on this day. And where Daguerre used cumbersome sheets of copper, Talbot invented a more flexible negative/positive paper process that needed much shorter exposure times – the Calotype process. Perhaps Daguerre got more headlines because he photographed some French ladies...

RUGBY KICKS OFF

26

Normally, picking up the football and running with it during a school game would get you a thumping from your teammates, but for English lad William Webb Ellis it earned him the reputation as the inventor of an entirely new sport – rugby. The first league was inaugurated today in 1871, and now millions of egg-chasers worldwide devote themselves to the game, which also influenced the development of American football, Canadian football and Australian rules football.

JETS TAKE OFF

27

Today we celebrate the man who is responsible for more happy holidays happening than anyone else. No, not Walt Disney – the Coventry-born engineering genius Sir Frank Whittle. On 27 January 1936, a company called Power Jets Ltd came into being. This little-known venture aimed to develop and manufacture Sir Frank's world-shrinking invention, the first ever jet engine. He succeeded, and it's been 'a small world after all' (to quote Walt Disney) ever since.

ROAD SAFETY GETS INTO GEAR

28 Petrol-heads won't be feeling very proud today, but the rest of us can be pleased. On this day in 1896, the first speeding conviction in history was handed out, to Walter Arnold of East Peckham. The speed limit was then 4mph in rural areas and just 2mph in towns – Arnold was clocked at a rip-snorting 8mph and fined one shilling plus costs. He could put his foot down later that year, though, when the speed limit was raised to a head-spinning 14mph.

NO, YOU CAN'T HAVE A BOAT

29 *Desert Island Discs* is an English cultural institution and the world's longest-running factual radio programme. It was first broadcast today in 1942, and its simple but intriguing format – famous people choose their eight favourite pieces of music, a book and a luxury item to be cast away with – became an instant hit. More than 22,000 discs have been chosen over the last 70 years, the most popular of which is Beethoven's 9th symphony. Mozart is the most requested composer overall (in case you thought it was Gary Barlow).

LYING IN STATE

30 Today in 1965 may have seen the end of Winston Churchill, but it was the beginning of his enduring legend. Born in Blenheim Palace, Churchill would become one of the greatest wartime leaders in history. He not only helped the Allies defeat the Axis powers in World War Two, but was also an eminent soldier, historian, artist and the only prime minister in the world to win the Nobel Prize for literature. He was one of the very few civilians ever to be given a state funeral and was the first person to be made an honorary citizen of the United States. More importantly, he also made it cool to flick the 'V' sign at people.

CUTTING EDGE CLINIC

31 England was the syphilis capital of the world in the 16th and 17th centuries, thanks to all those adventurers in their fancy ships sailing to parts unknown and bringing back God knows what in their breeches. Now that might not make you proud, but the fact that we then opened the world's first specialist venereal and tropical disease clinic to deal with the problem should. The London Lock Hospital was opened in Grosvenor Place on this day in 1747. Its name came from the 'locks', or rags, that lepers used to wear. Nice.

FEBRUARY

THOMAS OF ARABIA

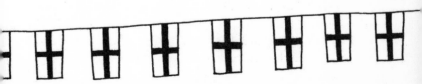

1 Thomas Edward (T.E.) Lawrence is one of the few men who has actually changed the world. After growing up and studying at Oxford, he became an archaeologist in the Middle East. When World War One broke out he became an intelligence officer thrust into the Arab fight against the Turks. Lawrence knew the Arabs' language, manners and mentality, and had the charisma and bravery to unite disparate tribes into a mighty guerrilla force. The Battle of Tafileh, fought today in 1918, saw the Turks routed and went down in history as Lawrence of Arabia's most brilliant feat of arms.

NO MAN IS AN ISLAND

The crew of the privateer *Duke* could hardly have thought they'd make literary history when they put in at the uninhabited island of Juan Fernandez, 420 miles off the coast of Chile, today in 1709. But they were astonished to be hallooed by a wild-looking bearded man dressed in goatskin and speaking English.

He was Alexander Selkirk, a sailor who had survived alone on the island for four years and four months. The castaway was almost incoherent with joy at seeing another human being. The crew returned Selkirk to England, where his life story became the basis for *Robinson Crusoe* by Daniel Defoe, the first ever novel written in English.

A VERY BRIGHT BOY

3

The saying '1 per cent inspiration, 99 per cent perspiration' is certainly true of Sunderland inventor Joseph Swan's route to success. Swan had the bright idea of the incandescent light bulb in 1850, but it wasn't until today in 1879 that he gave the world's first public demonstration of his invention in Newcastle upon Tyne. It was obviously better than gas lighting, and soon Mosley Street in Newcastle was the first public road in the world to be electrically lit (1880). Houses and theatres soon followed. Swan actually beat Thomas Edison by a year, but the pair quickly joined forces to turn their bulbs into bucks.

ACTION, ENGLISH-STYLE

4

Pinewood in Buckinghamshire went from a sleepy Victorian country house to one of the world's major movie studios. It its 75-year history, hundreds of celluloid classics have been shot there, including *Harry Potter*, the *Carry On* series, *Batman*, *Superman*, the *Bourne* franchise and most of the 23 James Bond adventures. *London Melody*, the first film made there, was released today in 1937. Together with Shepperton and Leavesden studios, Pinewood has helped London become the world's third busiest movie-making city, after LA and New York.

25

NICE NUGGET

5 The English have always had a knack for making big discoveries and, today in 1869, two Cornishmen made a whopper. John Deason and Richard Oates were mining near Moliagul in Australia when they dug up the world's largest gold nugget. It measured a mighty two feet by one foot and weighed 3,523.5 troy ounces. The canny Cornwall lads found it just 2 inches below the surface, by a tree root, and dubbed it the 'Welcome Stranger'. It earned them £9,000 – equivalent to £430,000 today, although it would be worth £2 million at today's gold prices.

SINGAPORE SLUNG

6 If you're going to start a colony it's always a good idea to do it somewhere warm where you can make lots of money by trading and amuse yourself by shooting wildlife. Well, that was Sir Thomas Stamford Raffles' plan anyway, when the Yorkshire-descended adventurer founded Singapore today in 1819. The famous Raffles Hotel is not only where the Singapore Sling was invented, it was where the last of the island's wild tigers was shot – in the Long Bar in 1902.

PIES, CHEESE AND POTS OF PAINT

7 Melton Mowbray is home to the world-famous pork pie, with the original pie shop established there today in 1851. It was the first town that was ever 'painted red'. In 1837, some drunk aristos were asked by the town's toll-keeper for payment. The gentlemen refused and, seizing some ladders and pots of red paint being used for gatehouse repairs, proceeded to paint the man. They then rampaged into town, painting a pub, the post office and a policeman. The next day, if you believe the locals, 'painting the town red' entered the English language.

FROM PILLAR TO POST

8 In the early 19th century, if you wanted to send a letter, you had to take it into the post office and hand it to the postmaster. The problem was particularly bad in the Channel Islands, thanks to weather, tides and irregular boat times. The Post Office sent a surveyor to find a solution. He had the ingenious notion of a 'letter-receiving pillar', octagonal and painted olive green. Guernsey installed its first three pillar boxes today in 1853. They were an instant success, and were adopted nationwide, painted red from 1874. The surveyor was Anthony Trollope, who would also go on to excel as a novelist.

POP TO THE TOP

9

Will Young or Gareth Gates? If you know what that question means, then you'll probably be interested to hear that the first TV *Pop Idol* was crowned tonight in 2002. The brainchild of English pop impresario Simon Fuller, the show went on to dominate Saturday night light entertainment TV all over the world, with countless international spin-offs and franchises. It also bequeathed its addictive format to global behemoth *The X Factor* – still one of the planet's most-watched TV shows.

WHAT THE DICKENS?

10

Charles Dickens is one of the world's best-selling novelists and the creator of some of the most memorable characters in literary history, including Oliver Twist, Ebenezer Scrooge, David Copperfield, Mr Micawber, Miss Havisham and Uriah Heep. There have been more than 180 film and TV adaptations of his works. The word 'Dickensian' has even entered the language and his stories, while as much a part of the English landscape as the white cliffs of Dover, seem to have an almost universal appeal. It was today in 1836 that Dickens' first novel *The Pickwick Papers* was commissioned as a monthly serial. It was an immediate success, bringing the 24-year-old writer instant fame.

SCI-FI HITS OUR SCREENS

11 Way back in 1938 on this day, BBC Television in London had an eye on the future when they produced the world's first ever science-fiction television programme. This was a 35-minute chunk of the Karel Capek play *R.U.R.*, set in a factory that makes artificial people. This play coined the term 'robot' – R.U.R. stands for Rossum's Universal Robots.

UNHAND OUR FISH, FROGGIES

12 England enjoys a generally good relationship with France (they have such lovely wine, after all), but occasionally they need to be taught a lesson. Take today in 1429, when an English force was quite innocently besieging the town of Orléans. The French then had the audacity to intercept a vital supply convoy of barrels of herring (admittedly, there might have been some crossbows and cannons in there too). This was simply too much. Seriously miffed by this misappropriation of their elevenses, our lads promptly won the resulting 'Battle of The Herrings'.

IN THE PINK

13

The Financial Times was first published today in London in 1888 as a four-page journal aimed at 'The Honest Financier and the Respectable Broker'. You might therefore wonder how it ever found a market, but it did. Its distinctive salmon-pink pages are now perused by half a million respectable (and perhaps a few not-so-respectable) moneymen every working day, making it the world's most influential business publication.

YE OLDE VALENTINE

14

'Romantic' might not be the most pre-eminent of English qualities, but the first recorded link of St Valentine's Day with romantic love is actually in Geoffrey Chaucer's *Parlement of Foules*, published in 1382. Furthermore, the practice of sending romantic cards to loved ones on this day first became widely popular in England in the late 18th century. Valentine's Day is now popular with lovers all around the world – and, let's be honest, with greetings-card companies.

DAN PULLS HIS WEIGHT

15 Daniel Albone from Biggleswade was a remarkable inventor who designed and built his own bicycle, complete with suspension, aged just 13. He created pioneering motorbikes, cars and the 'Ivel Agricultural Motor', which he patented today in 1902. This was the world's very first successful tractor. History does not record if Albone was also the first person to drive one of his inventions down a narrow country lane at 4mph on Bank Holiday Monday.

THE WINGS OF AN ANGEL

16 Although it met with quite a bit of resistance before it was built, Antony Gormley's *Angel of the North* has since become one of England's favourite landmarks. Construction of the 66-foot-tall steel sculpture was finished today in 1998. Its famous wings stretch for 177 feet and weigh 50 tonnes each. Locally the *Angel* is often affectionately referred to as the 'Gateshead Flasher'.

TURNING YOUR CAR INTO CASH

Not the most popular English innovation if you simply fancy driving around the capital's sights, but the London Congestion Charge (introduced today in 2003) has been one of the world's most successful such ventures. It has lowered accidents and emissions, and raised around £90 million a year to help fund Mayor Boris Johnson's other brilliant (or crackpot, depending on your point of view) schemes. Curiously, the US Embassy has refused to ever pay the charge, racking up £7.2 million of unpaid bills to the middle of 2013.

MAKING PROGRESS

The Pilgrim's Progress by Bedfordshire-born John Bunyan is one of the most famous and influential books in world literature and it was first published today in 1678. Its poignant Christian allegory has inspired countless other writers, been translated into more than 200 languages, and has never been out of print. Many of the characters, places and phrases have become proverbial, including the 'Slough of Despond', 'Vanity Fair', 'House Beautiful' and 'worldly wise'.

NEW YORK, NEW AMSTERDAM

19 Today in 1674 England and the Netherlands signed the Treaty of Westminster, ending the Third Anglo-Dutch War. It might sound like the end of an unremarkable – OK, boring – trade dispute but, crucially, it ceded the Dutch colony of New Netherland to England. Its then capital was lumbering under the awfully foreign name of New Amsterdam, but the city could now promptly be renamed New York in honour of its English owners. Much better.

PREMIER LEAGUE FORMED

20 The English Premier League is the world's most-watched soccer league and, in turn, the most lucrative. The idea first kicked off today in 1992 when clubs in the Football League First Division broke away from the Football League to take advantage of a juicy television rights deal. It's hardly the most egalitarian, though. Of the 46 clubs who have played in the Premiership, only five have won it: Manchester United, Arsenal, Chelsea, Manchester City and Blackburn Rovers.

BOUDICCA'S BONES

21

Warrior Queen Boudicca was one of the earliest of all English heroes, leading a major uprising against occupying Roman forces in AD 60. And today in 1988 archaeologists found what they think might have been her grave – under platform 8 at King's Cross station. Of course, it might just have been a commuter still waiting for the six o'clock to Peterborough, but it's a nice story.

BAA BAA CLONED SHEEP

22

You might think that, since sheep are hard enough to tell apart at the best of times, the last thing you want is two that are absolutely genetically identical. But today in 1997, a scientific team led by Warwickshire-born Sir Ian Wilmut announced the birth of Dolly the sheep – the world's first cloned mammal. With typically English 'Carry On' humour, she was named after Dolly Parton because the donor cell for the cloning procedure was taken from a mammary gland.

ONE JOLLY CAREFUL OWNER

23 In the days before eBay, people bought stuff they didn't really need (or ever use again, come to think of it) from classified adverts published in the back pages of newspapers. This whole concept is an English creation – the first such advertisement appeared today in 1886 in the pages of *The Times*. So we've been putting the class into classified for 128 years...

WATT A COPYCAT

24 You may know that Scotsman James Watt invented the device that would transform human existence more than any other innovation – the steam engine. Except he didn't. The atmospheric engine was the first machine that harnessed steam power to do work, and it was invented by Thomas Newcomen of Devon (born today in 1664). James Watt's more famous engine was an improved version of Newcomen's design, which had already been pumping water out of mines for over 50 years.

BRAVE, BRAVE MEN

25 The English-built ship *Birkenhead* sailed from Cape Town today in 1852 with 643 passengers – a mix of soldiers and civilian women and children. In the night the vessel struck an uncharted rock and began to sink. The commanding officer realised that rushing the lifeboats would swamp them and endanger the women and children, so he ordered his men to stand fast. Famously, they did. They landed all the women and children safely in the lifeboats, and almost all the men went down with the ship. Only 193 people survived. This heroic action is where the phrase 'women and children first' comes from, and still epitomises selfless, resolute bravery in the face of death. It is also known as the Birkenhead Drill.

FIRST GRAND NATIONAL RUN

26 Every year more than 500 million people tune in to watch their sweepstake pick blunder into the first hedge during the Grand National, the world's greatest steeplechase. The gruelling Aintree race covers 4 miles and 856 yards and throws up 30 fences. It was first run today in 1839 and was won, fittingly enough, by a horse called Lottery.

GOING UNDERGROUND

27

Early Tube maps were geographically correct, meaning central stations were crammed together, suburban ones were miles apart, and the lines swirled all over the place. Then Leyton-born draughtsman Harry Beck realised that travellers only needed to know the order of stations and where to change. He threw spatial correctness out of the window and simplified the lines into verticals, horizontals and diagonals. Today in 1933 saw the printing of his revolutionary Underground map. London got a new icon and the world got a design classic. Harry got 5 guineas.

THE SECRET OF LIFE...

28

Today in 1953, two Cambridge scientists wandered into the town's Eagle pub and announced, 'We have found the secret of life.' James Watson and Francis Crick weren't talking about best bitter (though they weren't far off!), they meant they had just decoded the structure of deoxyribonucleic acid (DNA to you and me). Their discovery that life's hereditary genetic information is structured in a double helix set the foundations for incredible advances in molecular biology, giving us greater understanding of the human body and how life is able to occur.

MARCH

'THE EAGLE' SOARS

1 With his bottle-end glasses, goofy grin and laughably abysmal ski-jumping, Eddie 'The Eagle' Edwards charmed the world at the Calgary Winter Olympics and returned home an English hero today in 1988. The Cheltenham-born athlete – sorry, plasterer – knew for a fact he wouldn't win when jumping, indeed might very well die, but still put absolutely every ounce of his effort into trying. Proper bulldog spirit. And his jumping may have been rubbish compared with gold medallist Matti Nykänen, but he was better than every single person in England had ever been at the event, setting a national record of 73.5m.

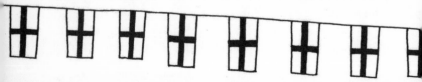

THE CO-OP OPENS ITS DOORS

Co-operative enterprises help people the world over afford goods and services they could not otherwise access. And, unlike banks, they don't charge you astronomical interest rates and then gamble all your money away. The prototype co-op was The Rochdale Society of Equitable Pioneers, founded in 1844. A group of 28 weavers and other artisans banded together to open a small store selling quality goods at a price the ordinary man could afford. It opened fully today in 1845 and was a huge success – within ten years there were 1,000 co-operatives across the country.

TO BE OR NOT TO BE ... THE BEST

William Shakespeare is widely regarded as not just the greatest writer in the English language, but also the world's pre-eminent dramatist. He is the best-selling author of all time, shifting around 4 billion copies of his plays and poetry. The earliest date we have for a production of one of his plays is today in 1592, when *Henry VI Part I* was first performed.

FOR THOSE IN PERIL ON THE SEA

4

The Royal National Lifeboat Institution (RNLI) was founded on this day in 1824. It was the idea of Yorkshireman Sir William Hillary, who believed a national lifeboat service manned by trained crews would be a huge benefit to seafarers and to the country. Smart thinking, considering that England and its islands have 6,261 miles of coastline and the weather does get awfully grumpy. Hillary was right – the RNLI's crews have saved over 137,000 lives over the years. In 2009, its fleet of 444 boats rescued an average of 22 people a day.

SPRAY TO GO

5

To some, he's a mindless vandal destroying the beauty of our cities; to others, he's a ground-breaking English artist who just happens to use public walls as his canvas. Who is he? Banksy, of course. Although the identity of the man with the can is one of the best-kept secrets in the art world, everyone is pretty sure he's from Bristol. Today his spray-painted rats, policemen, soldiers, apes and children are as likely to appear in Los Angeles, Berlin and New York as England. One of his most popular pieces was in the penguin enclosure at London Zoo, where he painted 'We're bored of fish' in 7-foot-high letters.

Banksy moved into filmmaking today in 2010 when his *Exit Through the Gift Shop* was released. It went on to be nominated for an Oscar. Banksy celebrated by painting a drunk Mickey Mouse on an LA billboard.

OUR NATIONAL (DRINKING) ANTHEM

The famously patriotic American national anthem, 'The Star-Spangled Banner', was inspired by the time British forces tried to burn revolutionary Baltimore to the ground. So it's ironic that the tune was originally a bawdy English drinking song written by John Stafford Smith of Gloucester. 'The Anacreontic Song' (published today in 1788) was the official song of The Anacreontic Society, a London gentlemen's club of amateur musicians who enjoyed a rousing singalong and a glass of red or three.

LECTURES WORTH ATTENDING

7 Many of today's great scientists had their love for the subject fired up by a Christmas lecture at the Royal Institution. Formed today in 1799 in Soho Square, London, with the specific purpose of 'diffusing knowledge', the Institution became world famous under the guidance of early lecturers Humphry Davy and Michael Faraday. One of its founders was Count Rumford, who also invented the modern fireplace, with its angled sides and tapering throat, which helps the fire burn more efficiently. And, vitally, he also devised the percolating coffee pot.

DON'T PANIC

8 *The Hitchhiker's Guide to the Galaxy*, by Douglas Adams, is uniquely English in its cosmic brand of whimsical lunacy and yet internationally loved. Pan-galactic gargleblasters, towels and the genius idea of the guide itself (which anticipated the smartphone 30 years before it became a reality) first graced this galaxy's airwaves today in 1978. It proved so popular it went on to become a series of books ('a trilogy in five parts', as Adams called it), a TV show, a blockbuster film and another radio series. Chances are we'll all still be raving about it when we are flying around in future spacecrafts of our own.

LONDON EYE OPENS

9

At 443 feet (135 metres) tall, the London Eye was the largest Ferris wheel in the world when it opened today in 2000. This unmistakable and much-loved landmark has 32 passenger pods (33 really, but pod 13 is always empty), representing London's 32 boroughs. Every year, nearly 4 million people step aboard to enjoy a pigeon's-eye view of the capital.

KATE GETS OUR VOTE

10

Women in England first got the vote in 1918, making us the seventh country to do so – not bad, but not brilliant. The first was New Zealand, in 1893. However, what's little known is that perhaps the most persuasive and powerful campaigner for suffrage in that country, Kate Sheppard, had been born (today in 1847) and brought up in Liverpool. A brilliant orator and organiser, she helped collect three enormous petitions, which ultimately led to full voting rights for women nine years before any other nation. Kate Sheppard appears on the New Zealand $10 note.

STREET OF SHAME

11 No newspapers are actually published in Fleet Street any more, but the name lives on as a general term for the industry. There had been book and legal publishers in the area since the early 16th century. Then, today in 1702, Edward Mallet published the *Daily Courant*, London's first daily newspaper, from premises above the White Hart Inn, establishing the trade for which the street would eventually become internationally famous. Or should that be infamous?

HOLY MOTHERS

12 The Church of England may have had a woman as its Supreme Governor for over 60 years (the Queen), but below her it was male priests all the way down until today in 1994, when the Church finally took the progressive (and, to some, controversial) step of ordaining its first women priests. According to a recent report, by the year 2025 there will be as many female priests as men. Currently, there are around 2,200 female priests and just under 4,500 male priests.

GROW UP AND BE COUNTED

13 Before this day in 1970, if you were a 20-year-old English youth, you could fight for your country, pay taxes, drink alcohol and get married – but not vote. Which seems a little unfair, considering you could die for your country in battle but not be counted in an election. But then, England became one of the first countries in the world to lower the voting age to the now-established 18. In Uzbekistan, for example, you still have to be over 25 to cast your ballot.

THIS IS GROUND CONTROL

14 The Jodrell Bank observatory in Cheshire has achieved many notable world firsts. Its Transit Telescope was the largest radio telescope in the world when it was built, and the Lovell Telescope was the largest steerable dish radio telescope in the world, at a mighty 250 feet in diameter. Lovell's vast motor system reused the gun-turret mechanisms from the battleships HMS *Revenge* and *Royal Sovereign*. But the observatory really made its mark on the world today in 1960, when it set a new record by establishing contact with the American Pioneer V satellite at a distance of 407,000 miles.

WHAT'S NEW, PUSSYCAT?

15 Yorkshireman Percy Shaw was driving home through dense fog, nearly veering off the road, when his headlights caught a cat sitting on the verge, and inspiration struck. The Reflecting Roadstud was inspired by the way the cat's eyes (invented millions of years ago by Mother Nature) reflected light back to the driver. Percy's company (opened for business today in 1935) produced millions of them during World War Two, when abrupt blackouts highlighted their value. He also later finessed his invention by adding a rainwater reservoir to the stud's base, making the glass eyes 'self-wiping' when a car drove over them.

POWER TO THE PEOPLE

16 With its distinctive four leg-like chimneys, Battersea Power Station has to be one of the world's strangest landmarks. Building started today in 1929, and the station was completed in two identical halves, twenty years apart. Despite now being little more than a shell, it is still the largest brick building in Europe. It has also, thanks in part to 70s rock band Pink Floyd, who featured it on an album cover, gone on to become an eerie industrial icon on the River Thames.

WOULD YOU ADAM AND EVE IT

17 Building the world's largest greenhouse in an old clay pit might seem a bit bonkers, but Tim Smit was a man with a vision. His Eden Project in Cornwall took two and a half years to construct but was a runaway success when it opened today in 2001, with a million people visiting every year. Its two biomes re-create rainforest and Mediterranean environments and contain 100,000 plant species from all around the world.

PASSED FIRST TIME

18 Today in 2007, fresh-faced Lewis Hamilton from Stevenage made his Formula One debut, in Australia for McLaren. He finished third. The next year he became the youngest Formula One World Champion, aged just 23, as he snatched the championship on the very last corner of the very last race. He was also the first black driver to win. Aged 10, Hamilton had said to the McLaren team principal, 'I want to race for you one day...I want to race for McLaren.' Within three years he was signed to their Young Driver Programme. Talk about knowing what you want in life...

MARTYRS TO A GOOD CAUSE

19 When six farm labourers from Tolpuddle, Dorset, were sentenced to transportation today in 1834, they can hardly have guessed they would be helping create the trade union movement. The Tolpuddle Martyrs simply wanted to protect their wages in the face of the rising mechanisation of farming. But they became popular heroes – 800,000 signatures were collected for their release and their supporters organised one of the first successful marches in the UK. All were eventually released.

PC PICKLES

England is famous for its brilliant fictional detectives, but when the coveted Jules Rimet Trophy, on display in Britain for the upcoming World Cup finals, was stolen today in 1966, the world hoped we could find a real one just as perceptive. No problem, old boy – up stepped Pickles, a black-and-white collie. This noble hound was out walking his human, David Corbett, today in South London when he sniffed an interesting parcel jammed under a hedge. Encouraging David to untie the parcel's string, Pickles was pleased to see that he had just sniffed out the stolen golden trophy. England went on to win the tournament for the first and only time. Pickles, sadly, died choking on his lead while chasing a cat.

LOOK, NO HANDS

Today in 1963 saw the introduction of a whole new generation of computer-controlled trains to the London Underground. These technological marvels led the world in their capabilities: they didn't need a driver to start, accelerate or to brake. They did, however, still require an operator on board for safety reasons, and to bellow 'Mind the gap!' repetitively at each and every station.

SCANDALISED

22 Here in England we like to do things properly – especially when it comes to sex scandals. And today in 1963, the greatest gaffe of the lot occurred when the Secretary of State for War, John Profumo, denied any impropriety with the model Christine Keeler. Of course, Profumo had been up to all sorts of naughty mischief, which was nearly a disaster because Christine was also linked romantically to a naval attaché at the Soviet Embassy. Profumo later resigned and the affair, along with both their careers, went down in infamy.

A VOTE FOR PROGRESS

23 This day in 1832 saw an important step on the journey towards modern democracy, with the passing of the Great Reform Act. Corruption in the electoral system was rife, with 'rotten boroughs' putting seats in landlords' pockets (the Duke of Norfolk controlled 11 constituencies). The new Act swept much of this away, giving fairer representation to larger populations and increasing the electorate from 400,000 to 650,000.

TIME TO SET SAIL

24 Determining longitude (how far east or west you were) was a thorny problem in the 18th century. Navigation errors led to many shipwrecks so, since sea trade was the key to world power, Parliament offered £20,000 (£2.87 million in today's money) as a prize for accurately measuring longitude. Then Yorkshire clockmaker John Harrison (born today in 1693) invented the marine chronometer, a timepiece accurate to within seconds on a transatlantic voyage. It revolutionised navigation, helping James Cook steer his way to Australia and Hawaii and ushering in a new era of ocean-going exploration.

THE GOOD CAPTAIN

25 Captain Thomas Coram was a shipbuilder and merchant who became dismayed at the number of abandoned babies he saw in London. So he set up the Foundling Hospital, which took in its first children today in 1741. It was the world's first incorporated charity. The original hospital in central London was demolished in the 1920s, but its site has since been turned into a children's play area, known as Coram's Fields.

BLAZING GOOD FUN

26 Fans of bright blazers and outrageously loud ties can take heart that the great Royal Regatta of Henley was founded today in 1839. The event, a very, very English affair and now an important date in the social calendar, was first organised by Captain Edmund Gardiner after seeing how popular the Oxford–Cambridge race had become. So, Gardiner proposed an annual regatta to 'be a source of amusement and gratification to the neighbourhood, and the public in general'. It has also been very influential: the instigator of the modern Olympics, Pierre de Coubertin, based the set-up of the International Olympic Committee on the Henley stewards.

WRAPPED AROUND HIS LITTLE FINGER

27 Shoelaces, as well as other various forms of attachments, had been stopping people's shoes falling off for centuries, but Englishman Harvey Kennedy's flash of inspiration was to physically patent the invention – basically two strings of leather – which he did today in 1790. Suffice to say, sales of his brainwave left him rather well-heeled.

YOU REAP WHAT YOU SOW

28 Jethro Tull, we salute you. No, not the band, although they are an English institution too. The original Jethro Tull (who was baptised today in 1674) was an agricultural pioneer who perfected a horse-drawn seed drill. Before Tull, seeds were broadcast by hand, a very inefficient and slow process. Tull's 1701 invention sowed the seeds in neat rows, raising production by as much as 800 per cent and helping to kick-start the Agricultural Revolution.

LIVE FROM KENSINGTON

29 The Royal Albert Hall is one of the most recognisable buildings in the world and it was opened by Queen Victoria today in 1871. The world's top performers in all artistic fields have graced its famous stage, from the Proms to Pink Floyd, Sumo wrestlers to school orchestras. It was so vast and impressive when built that unfortunately it had a noticeable echo. This was solved in 1969 with the installation of several large sound-diffusing mushrooms on the ceiling. Just look up and you'll see them.

FOREST FUN

30 There can be few more English ways to idle away an afternoon than by playing Pooh Sticks. Simply find a bridge over a lazy river, a friend and a stick each. Drop your sticks over the upstream railing then scurry over to the other side. The first stick to appear decides the winner. Then simply repeat until sundown (or you're called in for tea, whichever is sooner). The game was invented by Pooh author A.A. Milne and if you were passing Day's Lock on the River Thames today in 2014, you'd have seen the sport's annual World Championships. We take our fun very seriously in this country, you know.

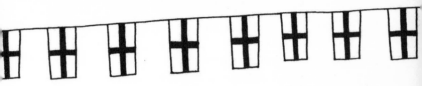

F FOR FLAMIN' FAST

31 The McLaren F1 is the supercar that left the rest of the world eating its dust. Designed and built in England, it set the record for the fastest road car in the world, clocking a whopping 240mph today in 1998. With a price tag of £540,000, it was then the most expensive car ever built, and as only 106 were ever made, it was also one of the most exclusive too.

APRIL

BOUNCING INTO HISTORY

Although the modern sport of bungee jumping was popularised in New Zealand, the very first elasticated jumps were made today in 1979 by five lads from the Oxford University Dangerous Sports Club, who decided it would be a good idea to tie their feet to a giant rubber band and jump off the 250-foot-high Clifton Suspension Bridge. As it transpired, it was bloody good fun and bungee jumping soon became the number one must-try adrenaline activity at exotic tourist locations around the world...as well as the odd car park in Swindon.

RADAR'S FIRST BLIP

2 In early 1935, the Air Ministry thought Nazi Germany might have a 'death ray' capable of flattening cities using radio waves, so they asked engineer Robert Watson-Watt to investigate. He concluded that the 'death ray' was an impossibility, but suggested that radio waves could be used to locate enemy aircraft. Just a few weeks later, he had built the world's first working model of such a system in a field outside Daventry, and today Watson-Watt received a patent for what would later become known as RADAR (Radio Detection and Ranging).

PUNK SPITS IN YOUR FACE

3 Punk rock might not be to your taste, but you can't deny that it was in genteel olde England that the genre roared into life. In 1976 London was *the* place to be if you were a phlegm-spitting, safety-pin-wearing, anti-Christ anarchist. And on this day in that year the Sex Pistols were supporting rock band the 101ers, whose lead singer was so blown away by the Pistols that he promptly decided punk was the future, left his band and went off to form a new group. He was Joe Strummer, his next band was the Clash, and their punk songs rocked the world...then spat in its face.

ZEBRA CROSSINGS INTRODUCED

4

There were designated pedestrian crossings before this day in 1949, but they were largely ignored by motorists and pedestrians alike. Then England brought the unmistakable zebra crossing into the world. There were 1,000 crossings at first, and their stripes were blue and yellow – not very Zebra-like. The world's most famous zebra crossing is the one featured on the cover of The Beatles' *Abbey Road* album in North London. It is perhaps the only traffic-safety feature that is also an international cultural landmark.

PASTORAL PIONEER

5 The Wirral might not leap to mind as one of the world's most inspiring natural environments. But as well as having acres of lovely lawns, lakes, trees, flower beds and winding paths, Birkenhead Park (opened today in 1847) is something of a groundbreaker. It was Britain's first publicly funded civic park, and its innovative design influenced many other beauty spots, in England and further afield. When American garden architect Frederick Law Olmsted strolled round the grounds in 1850, he was so thrilled that nine years later he copied most of its features and used them in his own masterpiece of landscaping – Central Park in New York.

HARRODS OPENS

6 Harrods (opened today in 1824) is surely the ultimate English shop. Famous for being a supplier of the finest of life's necessities, (and for selling things no one would ever need, but gosh, aren't they lovely), it is also the country's largest store by quite some distance. It covers five acres (about three football pitches) and has over one million square feet of selling space across 330 departments. Shame it's owned by Qatar, really.

IT'S TEA O'CLOCK

If you're one of the millions of English people who simply can't function before your morning cuppa, say a little 'thank you' this morning to Frank Clarke, a Birmingham gunsmith, who back in 1902 patented his 'Apparatus Whereby a Cup of Tea or Coffee is Automatically Made'. He later marketed this more snappily as 'A Clock That Makes Tea!' and so the first practical teasmade was born. Sadly fallen from fashion, one feels this most English of ingenious inventions is long overdue a comeback.

BARKING MAD

It was way back today in 1891 that Charles Cruft first held his eponymous dog show, and started a very English social event, at the Royal Agricultural Hall, Islington. On that day, there were 2,437 entries across 36 breeds. Now around 28,000 dogs enter Crufts each year, bringing 160,000 humans with them, making it the world's largest annual dog show (and the highlight of the year for poop-scoop manufacturers).

SUPERSONIC SUPERSTAR

9

The supersonic passenger jet Concorde was a glorious symbol of both English and (we have to grudgingly admit) French engineering excellence. And it was over our green and pleasant land that it first took to the skies, today in 1969, on its maiden flight from Filton, Bristol, to RAF Fairford, Gloucestershire. Since these places are only 37 miles apart, and the fancy jet could travel faster than the speed of sound, it probably didn't take very long. Still, a jolly fine achievement nonetheless.

THE WRITING OF COPYRIGHT

10

Before this day in 1710 the Stationers' Company (one of the Livery Companies of the City of London) had a monopoly on England's printing trade. All books had to be entered on their register, and only a Company member could do so; corruption and censorship were rife. Then the Statute of Anne introduced the world's first copyright legislation. Now publishers had 14 years' legal protection and the author was identified as the legal owner of the work.

IN THE BEGINNING WAS THE WORD

11 Getting bums on pews would be nigh-on impossible today if church services were all in Latin. But until William Tyndale translated the Bible into English, the word of God was indecipherable to the average person. Of course, in those days suggesting that the Bible should be available in, you know, the language we all speak, was punishable by being strangled and burned at the stake, which is how poor Tyndale met his maker. But just two years later, Henry VIII authorised The Great Bible, which used Tyndale's text. Published today in 1539, this first Bible in English is one of the most influential books ever written.

A VITAL BREAKTHROUGH IN TEAPOT TECHNOLOGY

12 Before William Cookworthy (born today in 1705) came along, tea in Europe was a drink enjoyed only by the upper classes. Porcelain, the preferred material for making teapots, was only made in China, pricing it out of most people's reach. Cookworthy – a sort of Robin Hood figure, but for tea – devised a way of making porcelain in Plymouth, helping everyone to enjoy a lovely cuppa. He was also one of the first people to suggest that sailors could avoid scurvy by eating fresh fruit and veg.

OFFICER CLASS

13 Established today in 1741, the Royal Military Academy at Woolwich was the factory for that indefatigable type of fighting Englishman, with a stiff upper lip and a never-say-die attitude. For nearly 200 years, until it closed in 1939, it trained the officers who would go on to shape our Empire. However, one of the surprise achievements of the Royal Military Academy was the invention of, somewhat bizarrely, the game of snooker – by a former Academy cadet in India in 1875.

MINI MARVELS

14 Small but perfectly formed – that's what made the Mini so beloved when it was launched today in 1959. It came into being because Leonard Lord, head of the British Motor Corporation, was irritated by all the cheap German cars on our roads: 'God damn these bloody awful bubble cars. We must drive them off the road by designing a proper miniature car!' And so he (or rather Alec Issigonis) did. Manufactured in their thousands at Longbridge and Cowley, when three Minis appeared as the getaway cars in the classic film *The Italian Job* in 1969, their iconic status was sealed.

WANDER AND WONDER

15

We've all seen a bed of spring daffodils and thought, 'Ooh, they're nice.' But few of us have turned that observation into a major literary movement. In fact, just one of us – William Wordsworth. He was out with his sister today in 1802 when he spotted the yellow flowers and promptly went off and wrote 'I Wandered Lonely as a Cloud'. It became his most famous work, helped to inspire the popularity of English romanticism and remains one of the world's best-loved poems.

THE CHEEKY CHAPPIE

16

In 1896, a seven-year-old boy was grubbing for existence in a London poorhouse. His mother was mentally ill and his father was on his way to dying of alcoholism. By 1918, he was the most famous man on the planet. Charles Spencer Chaplin (born today in 1889) escaped from his ferociously poor start in life to succeed first in vaudeville and then on film. He wrote, directed, produced, edited, composed the music for, and starred in most of his movies, with his tramp persona becoming a worldwide phenomenon. At 26 he was earning $670,000 a year, making him one of the highest-paid people in the world – a rags-to-riches tale too extreme for a cinema audience to believe!

ON YE ROAD

17 Today in 1397, Geoffrey Chaucer told his *Canterbury Tales* for the first time at the court of Richard II. Chaucer's poetic epic isn't just one of the major early works in English and a world literary classic, it's also the genesis of a genre that pervades today's teenage movies. For the adventures of the motley crew of tale-telling Canterbury pilgrims is surely the world's first road trip – complete with 14th-century debauchery, misadventure and hedonism as key themes.

PRESSED INTO ACTION

18 Extreme ironing – the sport that combines the thrills of a dangerous outdoor activity with the satisfaction of a well-pressed shirt – could only have been invented in England. Back in 2002 Phil Shaw combined extreme sport with tedious housework in Leicester, and thrill (and crease) seekers have since been snapped pressing their smalls on mountain tops, hanging from parachutes and even at the bottom of the ocean. But today in 2011 it got one of its crowning achievements when drivers on the M1 were astonished to see a man – in his dressing gown, of course – ironing a shirt on the southbound carriageway. Luckily the road had been temporarily closed, but still – eccentric in a very English way.

APRIL

IS ZIT IN IT?

19 After more than 70 years of scholarship, sweat and tears, today in 1928 saw the publication of the final section of the *Oxford English Dictionary*. It defined 600,000 words, the most of any world dictionary at the time, and extended to 12 volumes. More importantly, England's bored schoolboys could finally look up all the rude words beginning with Z.

TRIAL BY BATTLE

20 England's quirky laws are world famous, but this one was bonkers even by our standards. In 1817, Abraham Thornton was charged with the murder of Mary Ashford. He was acquitted, but Mary's brother, William Ashford, appealed and Thornton was rearrested. Thornton then pulled out two leather gauntlets and threw one down in the court, claiming the right to *trial by battle*. The court scratched its collective head, but this was Thornton's right under a medieval law relating to private appeals that had never been repealed, and his request was granted. Since Ashford declined the option of mortal combat, Thornton was freed on this day in 1818. The right to private appeals, and with that the right to trial by battle, was repealed the next year.

SUITS YOU, SIR

21 On this day in 1846, Henry Poole moved to Savile Row and started a trend for the street to be the international epitome of men's premier quality tailoring. Indeed, the word 'bespoke' originated on the street, from the reference to cloth that was said to 'be spoken for' by individual clientele. Henry Poole also invented the Tuxedo while on Savile Row. Originally made

APRIL

for the Prince of Wales in 1860, an American visitor took one of the classic tailored suits back to the US and caused a sensation when he wore it at the Tuxedo Club in upstate New York. To this day, Savile Row is still regarded as suit central – even if you don't see as many Tuxedos and top hats as you used to.

I AM SAILING

After 10 months alone at sea in his 32-foot boat *Suhaili*, Putney-born yachtsman Sir Robin Knox-Johnston sailed into Falmouth today in 1969 and became the first person to make a solo non-stop circumnavigation of the world. There were seven other sailors attempting the feat as part of a challenge laid down by the *Sunday Times*, but one by one they all dropped out, leaving Knox-Johnston the only finisher. Wouldn't have fancied doing his laundry after a trip like that...

ST GEORGE'S DAY

As patron saints go, St George doesn't really inspire much in the way of national celebration, certainly compared with, say, St Patrick. Maybe this is because he wasn't actually English, but a Roman soldier who was born in Syria. Nonetheless, his cross is the basis of our national flag, so today why not go out and chase a dragon or two in his honour? Curiously, St George is also the patron saint of those suffering from syphilis. He certainly deserves a clap for that.

THESE BOOTS ARE MADE FOR WALKING

It's a historic day for those of us who love the great English outdoors – today in 1965, the Pennine Way was formally opened. One of our most challenging long-distance trails, it stretches for 267 glorious miles from Edale in the Peak District, north through the Yorkshire Dales and the Northumberland National Park, traversing the very backbone of England.

GET YOURSELF IN THE PICTURE

Since it first opened on this day in 1769, The Royal Academy's Summer Exhibition in Piccadilly has shown off the work of some of England's greatest artists, including Turner, Gainsborough and Hockney. But the truly wonderful thing is that the exhibition is open to everyone – if you've done a nice picture of your cat using poster paints, you are welcome to enter it. Just pay your £25 fee and send it in.

THE MARK OF QUALITY

When several prominent civil engineers met today in 1901 under the leadership of English engineer Sir John Wolfe-Barry (who designed Tower Bridge), they wanted to standardise steel sizes for industry. This 'Engineering Standards Committee' was successful, cutting the number of tramway rail gauges from 75 to 5 and saving millions. The committee later became the British Standards Institution and their famous Kitemark® became a stamp of quality recognised worldwide. Have a look at any car window or fire extinguisher in the country and you'll see this famous symbol.

PALACE OF WESTMINSTER STARTED

The site of the Houses of Parliament was originally a palace for English royals, first established in the 11th century. Kings and queens lived at Westminster until a fire gutted the complex in 1512. Parliament then took over but, in 1834, an even greater fire destroyed the buildings. A national competition to design a replacement parliament building was won by Charles Barry's gothic pile. Today in 1840, the foundation stone was laid for the rebuilding of Westminster, the building that would come to symbolise England's power, history and heritage more than any other.

BLIGH'S REVENGE

28

The famous Mutiny on the Bounty, which happened today in 1789, has long been portrayed as Fletcher Christian's courageous uprising against the tyrant William Bligh. But Cornishman Bligh wasn't so harsh by the standards of the day, and he was one of the most phenomenal sailors England has ever produced. Cast adrift in an open boat with no instruments, he navigated 3,618 nautical miles of tumultuous seas to reach safety. The mutineers mostly ended up killing each other.

KATE & WILL TIE THE WINDSOR KNOT

29

Today in 2011, our country (and much of the rest of the world) came to a halt to watch a young English couple tie the knot and make a fairytale come true. Well, a large number of men actually took to the golf course, but still, the marriage of Prince William to 'commoner' Catherine Middleton was a wonderful occasion that sparked the biggest celebrations in years. The country enjoyed a national holiday, street parties (with government-funded bunting) and blanket TV coverage of the entire day – especially Kate's dress. And yes, the new Duchess of Cambridge did look lovely.

HANDY LANDY

30

The Land Rover – a beacon of English car manufacturing – was built to be the toughest thing on four wheels, and was an instant hit with hardy-car lovers when it debuted at the Amsterdam Motor Show today in 1948. Farmers could plough fields with the Solihull-built beauties, the Army could happily drop them out of planes, and explorers could run their 'Landy' for a few thousand miles on banana oil if that's all they had to hand. Sixty years later, around 70 per cent of all Land Rovers ever built are still chugging through the world's bogs, deserts, jungles and suburbs.

MAY

A TRULY GREAT EXHIBITION

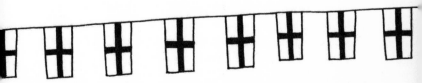

The Great Exhibition of 1851, which was opened today by Queen Victoria, was intended as a magnificent advertisement of England's, and her Empire's, industrial and artistic prowess. It featured exhibits from all over the world, but pride of place was given to home-grown wonders. In its six-month run, 6 million people – equivalent to a third of the entire population of Britain at the time – visited the exhibition. Its £186,000 (£16,190,000 today) profit was used to found the now world-renowned Victoria and Albert Museum, the Science Museum and the Natural History Museum. A *slightly* more impressive legacy than the Millennium Dome.

HEAVEN'S BELLS

2 The glorious sound of church bells ringing out is, for many, the archetypal soundtrack of the English village. Change ringing is the art of ringing a set of church bells in a series of intricate patterns or 'changes'. Accomplishing a full 'peal' of bells – a pattern of a set length that has no repeated changes – is a prodigious feat of concentration and physical effort. The first true peal happened today back in 1715 at the 14-bell church of St Peter Mancroft in Norwich. The ringers went through 5,040 changes of a pattern called 'Plain Bob Triples'.

DRAMA KING

3 As theatre impresarios go, it takes a lot to beat Richard D'Oyly Carte (born today in 1844). He rose from a humble start in Soho to become a composer and musician. He then worked as a talent agent, and had Matthew Arnold and Oscar Wilde on his books. To realise his dream of high-quality English comic opera that the whole family could enjoy, he brought together dramatist W.S. Gilbert and composer Arthur Sullivan. He then founded his eponymous theatre company to stage their very successful productions. With his profits he built two theatres and the country's first luxury hotel, the Savoy.

ROYCE MEETS ROLLS

4 England has long had a reputation of making some of the best cars on the planet, and the most famous of all the top-class manufacturers has to be Rolls-Royce. Well, Charles Rolls and Henry Royce met for the first time today in 1904 at the Midland Hotel in Manchester and agreed to work together, with the simple aim of producing the finest motor cars in the world. Their uncompromising pursuit of quality has attracted a loyal following among the planet's rich and famous. An eclectic mix of Rolls-Royce fans includes General Franco, John Lennon, Brigitte Bardot, Sylvester Stallone, P. Diddy, Alan Sugar and Elvis Presley.

HOSTAGES FREED – LIVE ON TV!

5 The SAS had existed as a special forces regiment since 1941, but it was their starring role in the Iranian Embassy siege in London today in 1980 that brought them to the world's attention. Terrorists had seized the embassy on 30 April, and had just shot a hostage when the SAS stormed the building live on TV. Abseiling onto balconies from the roof, they used frame charges and stun grenades to blast their way in, before killing five of the six militants and rescuing nineteen hostages.

GILBERT SCOTT FINDS HIS CALLING

6 The red phone box is a design classic, but it was actually the sixth attempt at creating a national phone booth. London-born architect Giles Gilbert Scott – also responsible for iconic English buildings Liverpool Cathedral, Waterloo Bridge and Battersea Power Station (see 16 March) – won a competition to create the box and his K6 (kiosk number six) design was rolled out today in 1935. There were 73,000 in Britain by 1980 and, although many have since been replaced, around 2,000 now have listed status.

THINKING SMALL

7 Today in 1952, electronics engineer Geoffrey Dummer from Hull presented the first public description of an integrated circuit, or microchip. His conceptual breakthrough was to visualise electronic equipment as a solid block of conducting material with no connecting wires. Components could then be smaller and more reliable, marking a giant step towards *Grand Theft Auto*. Well, modern computers, anyway.

TURNING THE TIDE

8 London has always been vulnerable to flooding, but 1953's huge North Sea storm focused the minds of the powers that be into taking action. And after years of study, discussion and construction, the Thames Barrier was finally opened today in 1984. This engineering marvel is raised when a predicted storm surge combines with unfavourable tides and river flow, preventing the flood waters inundating the capital. Those who doubt climate change is happening may like to note that the barrier was raised 4 times in the 1980s, 35 times in the 1990s and 75 times in the 2000s...

THAT'S THE WAY TO DO IT!

9 The PC brigade may have tried to stamp out its husband-beating, baby-dropping, crocodile-killing fun, but the traditional English Punch and Judy show is once again popular. The figure of Punch made his English debut in Covent Garden today in 1662, as recorded by diarist Samuel Pepys. The figure of Punch came from the Italian trickster character of Pulcinella, and the show was originally very much aimed at adults. By Victorian times it was more child-friendly (if still very violent) and youngsters have been 'pleased as Punch' ever since.

ART FOR ALL

10 Our National Gallery isn't the world's biggest (that's the State Hermitage museum in Russia) but it is splendid and, importantly, free to enter since it first opened today in 1824. Originally sited in a townhouse at No. 100 Pall Mall with just 38 paintings, this soon became far too small as the collection grew, and in 1832 construction began on a landmark building in the then-new Trafalgar Square. To this day it is still one of London's top draws for tourists.

LOTSA LOOS

A statue of the 1966 World Cup-winning captain Bobby Moore was unveiled today in 2007, marking the opening of the new home of English football, the rebuilt Wembley stadium. This magnificent arena is not just the most capacious in Britain (90,000) and one of the largest in the world; it also boasts the most lavatories of any venue anywhere – 2,618, to be exact.

PLASTIC FANTASTIC

Today in 1862, Birmingham inventor Alexander Parkes displayed the world's first plastic at the 1862 London International Exhibition. He modestly called it Parkesine (well you would, wouldn't you?), but it would later be developed as celluloid. Parkes' plastic enabled photographs to be produced on a flexible material (rather than glass or metal), effectively making motion pictures possible.

A CRIMINALLY GOOD DEAL

13 Today in 1787 eleven ships crammed with convicts left to establish a penal colony in Australia – the first European settlement down under. Shipping your convicts off to the other side of the world was a simply brilliant idea. You no longer had to feed and clothe them and they couldn't escape and start nicking things again. It was even more awesome for the convicts: 'Let me get this straight – you want me to leave this dingy, rat-infested, filth-strewn cell in the basement of Newgate Prison and go to…Botany Bay? Er, yes.' No wonder there was so much crime in 19th-century England – they were all desperate to be transported.

JENNER JOUSTS WITH SMALLPOX

14 In 1796, smallpox killed around 400,000 people a year in Europe alone. Then Gloucestershire-born scientist Edward Jenner learned that milkmaids who caught the cowpox virus (a similar, less virulent disease) did not catch smallpox. Today, he inoculated his gardener's eight-year-old son (well volunteered, young man) with material from the cowpox blisters of the hand of a milkmaid, and in doing so created the world's first vaccine. In 1979, thanks to mass vaccination, smallpox was declared eradicated worldwide. As the 'father of immunisation', Jenner's ingenious discovery has probably saved more lives than any other.

SQUARE SHOT IN A ROUND HOLE

15 The Puckle gun, patented today in 1718 by London inventor James Puckle, was the world's first machine gun. That's not a very nice thing to boast about, but the invention itself was at least eccentric in a very English way: it could fire round shot at 'civilised' enemies and square shot at Turks. Puckle reasoned that since the square shot caused more damage, this would convince the Turks of the benefits of our Christian 'civilisation'.

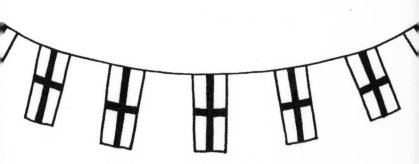

THE BIGGEST BALLOON

16 Designed to zip the length and breadth of the British Empire, the *R101* airship was the world's largest flying craft when completed today in 1930. It captured the world's imagination, but crashed on its maiden flight, a giant balloon of flammable hydrogen not proving to be the most manoeuvrable or safe of aircraft. The vast shed in Bedfordshire in which the *R101* was built was the largest building in Britain, and today it is the largest enclosed laboratory in the world. Its twin shed still builds airships today, but these are smaller and much, much safer.

LIGHTING UP OUR LIVES

17 Next time you come home from work, grab a beer and relax in your sunshine-filled garden, thank William Willett from Chislehurst. He was out riding early this morning in 1907 when he noticed how many blinds were still down, and he had the bright idea for daylight saving time. He published a pamphlet 'The Waste of Daylight', which proposed advancing clocks at the start of summer to save electricity and gain evening light. When the First World War brought an urgent need to save coal, Britain finally introduced the scheme. Many other countries soon copied the clock-changing, beer-enjoying idea.

BEST EVER MOUSE CATCHER

18

No, we didn't invent the cat. But James Henry Atkinson from Leeds did invent the Little Nipper Mousetrap (trademarked today in 1909). This murderous machine is a design classic. Made of wood and wire, it is cheap and very effective – it slams shut in just 0.038 of a second, faster than any other trap. The Patent Office holds designs for over 4,400 mousetraps, but the Little Nipper still dispatches around 60 per cent of the world's trapped mice to the great cheese cupboard in the sky.

THESE GO UP TO 11...

19

In the early 1960s Jim Marshall was running a drum shop in West London when he started importing guitars and amps. His customers (who happened to include Eric Clapton and Jimi Hendrix) wanted a louder sound, so he founded Marshall Amplification today in 1964. His first masterstroke was the revolutionary JTM45 50-watt amp. When the musicians demanded even more oomph, Jim piled up the amplifiers on top of each other, creating the speaker stack. This tower of power became a must-have for all hard-rocking stars, and Marshall is still one of the most popular and iconic brands of amplifier in the world. Jim became known as 'The Father of Loud'.

PROPER PEARLIES

20

The first Pearly King was Henry Croft, a Victorian rat-catcher. London's costermongers (street fruit-sellers) then wore suits decorated with pearl buttons on the seams. Henry went one step further and completely covered a suit in pearls, including top hat and tails. He became famous and used his celebrity to raise money for charity. His colourful look and voluntary work is continued by the 'Pearlies' who today hold their annual Memorial Service in Trafalgar Square.

CANAL DREAMS

21

In the late 19th century, the high dues charged by the Port of Liverpool led developers to plan a large canal reaching from the sea right into the heart of the industrial powerhouse of Manchester. After six years of construction, the Manchester Ship Canal was opened by Queen Victoria today in 1894. This 36-mile engineering marvel was then the world's largest navigation canal. It still carries about 6 million tons of freight each year.

WEAVING WONDERS

22 Before John Kay from Lancashire patented his flying shuttle today in 1733, weavers could only produce pieces of cloth as wide as their arms, since they had to pass the shuttle that held the thread from hand to hand. But Kay's ingenious invention was wheeled and pointed, allowing weavers to shoot it faster across a much wider bed of fabric. Weaving became more efficient and hugely more profitable, helping to drive the Industrial Revolution in England.

LONDON ORBITAL

23 Where do you suppose is the headquarters of the most advanced international satellite technology? CERN? Cape Canaveral? MIT? Actually, it's Stephenson Road, a cul-de-sac behind the Holiday Inn, Guildford, where Surrey Satellite Technology (formed today in 1985) is based. Starting as a research project run by the University of Surrey, SST grew to become the world's leading manufacturer of small satellites. To date, they have had 41 successful launches. Alas, these do not take place from their Guildford offices, but usually from the Baikonur cosmodrome in Kazakhstan.

CHOCOLATE CAN BE GOOD FOR YOU

24 Kitkat, Smarties, Aero, Black Magic, Fruit Gums and Fruit Pastilles – if you've ever enjoyed them (so that's everyone, then) you can be proud of Joseph Rowntree from York (born today in 1836). His brilliant ideas for sweet products and factory techniques helped him grow his brother's company from 30 to 4,000 employees. But he also seemed to genuinely think that it might be a nice idea to treat his workforce fairly. He gave much of his money to charity and set up several reforming trusts that are still going today. Rowntree founded the world's first occupational pension scheme.

ROYAL SEAL OF APPROVAL

25 Having a Royal Warrant above your shop door is a sure sign of high quality (and perhaps of high prices, now that we think about it), and some of the best English manufacturers display them. Henry II gave the first Royal Charter to the Weavers' Company in 1155, and the practice flourished, particularly in Victorian times. Today in 1840 the Royal Tradesmen's Association was formed to help promote the 'best of the best', and there are now around 850 Royal Warrant holders, ranging from Aston Martin to Tom Smith's Christmas crackers.

DEEPEST BLUE

Almost nothing was known about the ocean deeps until the landmark study carried out by scientists aboard HMS *Challenger*, which arrived back home at Spithead in Hampshire today in 1876. This ship was converted into a floating laboratory for its epic four-year voyage of 68,890 nautical miles. The scientists took thousands of measurements and samples to get the first real view of major seafloor features. They discovered more than 4,700 new species and laid the groundwork for the entire discipline of oceanography. They also first sounded the deepest part of the world's oceans, paying out 4,475 fathoms (26,850ft) of line before touching bottom in the area now known as the Challenger Deep.

CHELSEA FLOWER SHOW

Officially it is known as the Great Spring Show, but to most English garden fans it is simply the Chelsea Flower Show, the most famous horticultural event in the world. First held today in 1862, it gives gardeners the chance to catch the latest plant trends in what is a virtual catwalk for the gardening world. It is also simply very beautiful, and every year 157,000 visitors come to check out the tulips.

OPEN-HOUSE OPERA

28 Glyndebourne festival is an annual English institution. Family-run and financially independent, the festival is like no other on Earth – think Glastonbury but for toffs instead of commoners. It's *the* music festival, and date in your social calendar, to be seen at, where opera and classical music fit the bill. Well-heeled music lovers in fancy evening dress have flocked to enjoy classical sounds at this country pad/opera house since the first festival opened today in 1934 with a performance of Mozart's *Le Nozze di Figaro*.

THE TIME MACHINE ARRIVES IN THE PRESENT

29 H.G. Wells was one of the few English writers influential enough to create an entire genre. His first novel, *The Time Machine*, was published in Britain today in 1895, and he went on to write many more sci-fi classics, including *The Island of Doctor Moreau*, *The Invisible Man*, *The War of the Worlds* and *The First Men in the Moon*. Before writing professionally, Wells was a teacher. One of his pupils was A.A. Milne, future creator of another English literary icon, Winnie the Pooh.

MAKING MONEY IS CHILD'S PLAY

30 Frank Hornby was a Liverpool bookkeeper who in his spare time made mechanical toys for his sons with pieces cut out from sheet metal. After scrabbling together some money he marketed the little engineering kits he made. Kids lapped them up, and so Frank founded Meccano Ltd on this day in 1908, which eventually made him a rich man. And he wasn't finished inventing classic English toys – for an encore he created Dinky Toys and gave his name to the national treasure that is the Hornby model railway system.

HEATHROW AIRPORT TAKES OFF

31 Heathrow Airport (which opened today in 1946) may be the world's busiest international airport, but we all know it's not exactly a place that instils national pride. And yet maybe that's the point: it shows a certain confidence in the rest of our country that we're prepared to let visitors' first view of England be a cramped concrete warren of lost luggage, oleaginous burger joints and countless queues full of exhausted and despairing travellers who just want to be anywhere else but there. Welcome to England!

JUNE

A MAGNETIC PERSONALITY

It's hard enough finding the North Magnetic Pole nowadays – the pesky thing moves 35 miles a year. Back in 1831 it took a very intrepid gentleman from London by the name of James Clark Ross to pin it down on this day as it meandered across the wastes of northern Canada. Ross was a truly great English explorer whose name is attached to a rather large area of the world: the Ross Sea in Antarctica is named after him, as is the Ross Ice Shelf and Ross Island. He also discovered Mount Erebus and Mount Terror, two Antarctic volcanoes.

SHE TAKES THE TOP JOB

Elizabeth Alexandra Mary is the full name of a London girl who today in 1953 got herself one heck of a promotion. At the age of just 25, young Liz suddenly became Queen Elizabeth II, monarch of England, the United Kingdom, Supreme Governor of the Church of England, queen of 16 independent sovereign states, the figurehead of the 54-member Commonwealth of Nations and later the patron of over 600 charities and other organisations. How she finds the time to walk her corgis I don't know. Gawd bless her!

IT LIVES...

The blood-curdling tale of the monster created from spare body parts and galvanised into life by Victor Frankenstein is one of the most haunting and influential stories of all time. Even more remarkable is the fact that *Frankenstein*; or, *The Modern Prometheus* was written by an 18-year-old London girl, Mary Shelley. She spent the wet summer of 1816 with the poet Percy Shelley and Lord Byron, each writing stories for the others' amusement. Mary picked up her pen and gave life to a monster... and a legend. In the book Frankenstein's monster is never given a name, though Shelley herself did refer to it as...Adam.

RALEIGH REALLY IN A HURRY

4 Sir Walter Raleigh epitomised the English hero who jolly well just got on with things. He founded the first English colony in North Carolina today in 1584, mounted not one but two expeditions to find the fabled city of El Dorado, and popularised tobacco in England. Raleigh also commissioned the first *Ark Royal* and planted the first potatoes in Ireland. As he was summoned to the executioner's block for conspiring against King James I, his last words as he lay his head down were: 'Strike, man! Strike!' Stiff upper lip or what!

MARKS & SPARKS

5 Despite various financial wobbles, Marks & Spencer is still one of England's most beloved shops. It was founded in 1884 when Michael Marks, from Poland, and Thomas Spencer, a cashier from Yorkshire, set up a stall in Kirkgate Market, Leeds. Until 2002, Marks & Spencer only sold British-made goods, and its 'St Michael' brand (introduced today in 1928) was a symbol of quality and value for money. Curiously, there was an M&S in Kabul in the 1960s. What the Afghans thought of its best brandy-laced Christmas pudding is anyone's guess.

YOU CAN DO WHATEVER YOU FEEL

A cowboy, a construction worker, a biker, a police officer, a soldier and a native American got together in London today in 1844 to found one of the world's great social aid institutions – the YMCA. Well, not quite. Actually, it was George Williams, a draper from Somerset. He was shocked by the terrible living conditions of young country lads like himself who had come to find work in London. So he created a safe, Christian place for them to stay, far from the temptations of alcohol, gambling and handlebar moustaches. Today the YMCA helps more than 58 million people every year.

DEDICATED FORERUNNER OF FASHION

Beau Brummell (born in London today in 1778) was a famous dandy of Regency England who established the gentlemen's fashion of tailored dark suits with full-length trousers worn with a cravat. He claimed it took him five hours to dress and that he polished his boots with champagne. That might sound ridiculous, but it's thanks to him that people all over the world wear a suit with a tie. Beau established and championed this good-looking combination and it soon became the fashion of the day. Way to go, Beau.

WEDGWOOD SERVED UP TO ROYALTY

8 Josiah Wedgwood was an unlikely candidate to be the 'Father of English Potters'. Smallpox left him with a bad leg that was later amputated, making it impossible for him to even turn a potter's wheel. But when he perfected an elegant cream-coloured earthenware, it earned royal approval (today in 1766) and this 'Queen's Ware' established his fame, which grew rapidly. So too did his fortune, thanks to his extraordinary marketing nous: direct mail, money-back guarantees, the travelling salesmen, self-service, free delivery, buy-one-get-one-free, illustrated catalogues; they *all* came from Josiah Wedgwood.

TOUCHING HEAVEN

9 Everyone knows that the first man to stand on top of Mount Everest was New Zealander Sir Edmund Hillary in 1953 – or was it? It may very well have been Englishman George Mallory, on this day 29 years earlier. Mallory was a brilliant mountaineer who had already twice come close to surmounting the ultimate summit. On the third attempt he and his climbing partner, Cheshire-born Andrew 'Sandy' Irvine, were last seen alive just 800 feet (245m) below the summit ridge, before storm clouds shrouded them forever.

RACING INTO HISTORY

10 The first University Boat Race took place on this day in 1829 at Henley-on-Thames. The Boat Race is one of the most famous sporting events in the world, with millions watching every year on TV and around 250,000 lining the riverbank. It's also a notoriously tough race, being held no matter how nasty the conditions. Cambridge sank in 1859 and 1978, Oxford in 1925 and 1951, and both boats went down in 1912. The main difficulty in 2012 was protestor Trenton Oldfield, who decided it was a good idea to jump into the Thames and buzz the boats.

THIS VACUUM SUCKS

11 He wasn't the first person to realise that most vacuum cleaners just moved the dirt around rather than actually sucking it up, but James Dyson was the one who did most about it. The Norfolk-born inventor realised that a bagless system based on the cyclones that clean dust out of sawmills could work. He built 5,127 prototypes before developing a model that worked. Even then, manufacturers turned their noses up – it would ruin the market for bags. So today in 1993 Dyson opened his own factory, and 14 years after he started trying he got his first product into a shop. It's now a design classic.

ALL THE WORLD'S A STAGE

12 It took 27 years of planning and four of construction, but the replica of Shakespeare's world-famous Globe theatre on the South Bank finally opened today in 1997 with a performance of *Henry V*. It's as close to the original circular playhouse as possible: made of English oak, it has a thrust stage, three tiers of steep seating, space for 700 'groundlings', and the first and only thatched roof permitted in London since the Great Fire of 1666.

LOVE/HATE RELATIONSHIP

13 There are different versions of Marmite around the world, but only the English one makes the roof of your mouth feel like you've just snorted gunpowder. If you're a fan of that feeling then you ought to know that The Marmite Food Extract Company was formed today in 1902 in Burton upon Trent. This famous brewing town was chosen because concocting the yeasty spread demands beer-making by-products. Incidentally, Marmite isn't only good for spreading on toast – in the 1930s English scientist Lucy Wills used it to identify the beneficial effects of folic acid.

HERE'S LISTENING TO YOU, KID ...

14 In early 1931, Hampstead-born electrical engineer Alan Blumlein went to see a film with his wife. Cinemas then only had a single set of speakers, and Blumlein thought it unacceptable that the actor's voice came from the left when his face was on the right-hand side of the screen. He had a point. Blumlein then told his wife that he would fix that problem and promptly went back to his lab and invented stereo sound, which he patented on this day of that same year. The worlds of cinema and music would never sound the same again.

RIGHTS ARE WRITTEN

15 King John may have been a hopeless King of England, but he did do one very, very important thing on this day in 1215, when he attached his Great Seal to the Magna Carta at Runnymede. This historic document started as a cunning ploy by ambitious barons to weaken the King, but it also gave English people some important rights. Several are still on the statute books today, including the very important idea that no 'freeman' can be punished except following a trial by his peers. The Magna Carta also influenced the constitutions of many other countries, including the United States.

GERMANY'S (ENGLISH) ECONOMIC MIRACLE

16

Although the first Volkswagen factory was founded by a certain Mr Adolf Hitler to produce Beetles, the company wouldn't exist today if it weren't for Yorkshire-born Major Ivan Hirst. At the end of the war, the bomb-damaged plant was going to be scrapped. Then Major Hirst took charge, today in 1945. He knew that the occupying British Army were short of vehicles, and this would be the perfect place to build them. Cars were cobbled together from whatever old stock was around, using machinery found hidden in outhouses. By 1946, 1,000 cars a month were rolling off the production lines. Today Volkswagen is the world's largest automotive company. If only Hirst had been put in charge of Rover.

FREE THINKER

17

While travelling from Cambridge to London, most of us would be thinking about what to have for lunch, or whether we'd put the cat out. Thomas Clarkson from Wisbech, however, was cogitating on this day in 1785 on the far loftier notion of how to abolish the slave trade. After having an epiphany on the road, he published an essay he'd written at university, which caught the attention of other abolitionists and MP William

Wilberforce. Together they helped pass the Slave Trade Act of 1807, which ended British trade in slaves. Clarkson went on to campaign successfully in Europe and America.

NOT ON YOUR LIFE

18 The first life insurance policy as we know it was taken out today in 1583 by an English salter named William Gibbons. It is notable because, even then, the underwriters tried to wriggle out of paying. The term was 12 months and Gibbons duly died within that period, on 29 May 1584. But his heirs were astonished to hear the underwriters claim that 'month' meant a period of 28 days, and so the policy had expired. It went all the way to court before Mr Gibbons was favoured.

BOBBIES ON THE BEAT

19 Before this day in 1829, law and order in London was maintained by volunteer constables and watchmen. Home Secretary Sir Robert Peel recommended a new style of police force: an official, paid profession, organised in a civilian rather than military way. Crucially, it should also be answerable to the public. And so the world's first modern police force was born.

VICTORIA REIGNS SUPREME

20 When Queen Victoria succeeded to the throne today in 1837 it was one of the most significant moments in English history. Just 18 when crowned, she reigned for 63 years and 7 months, longer than any other British monarch and the longest of any female monarch ever. The Victorian era saw a flourishing of industry, culture and science, as well as the expansion of the British Empire, which eventually covered around a quarter of the planet.

WHAT'S THIS RIVER DOING HERE?

21 Before all this new-fangled GPS technology, we relied on Ordnance Survey maps to get us lost in the middle of Dartmoor. And the historic map-making experts have been helping English travellers mislay perfectly good paths since this day in 1791. The government, wary of invasion from revolutionary France, instructed the Board of Ordnance to accurately survey the south coast of England. Having successfully mapped Kent at one-inch-to-the-mile by 1801, the OS went on to map the whole of Britain, which took more than twenty years. It was the first national topographic survey in the world. The survey's five-mile baseline was on Hounslow Heath, now part of Heathrow Airport.

HOWZAT!?

Lord's (named after its founder, Thomas Lord) is the spiritual home of world cricket. The ground hosted its first match today in 1814, between Marylebone Cricket Club and Hertfordshire. Lord's also has the world's oldest sporting museum, which contains hundreds of years of celebrated cricket memorabilia, including the Ashes urn (the one the players hold up is a replica). The actual pitch is also remarkable because it has a significant slope: the northwest side of the ground is eight feet higher than the southeast side.

IDLE SPECULATION

'It is folly to allow decadent and selfish speculators too much influence,' said John Maynard Keynes, and for decades, governments listened. The Cambridge-born economist was one of the 20th century's most influential people, and so smart he apparently made Bertrand Russell feel like a fool. 'Keynesian' theories suggesting the state should intervene to avoid 'boom and bust' cycles shaped the recovering Western economies after World War Two. He also helped establish the World Bank and the International Monetary Fund. He was made a peer today in 1942. His ideas fell from favour in the 70s and 80s, but after the 2008 financial crisis, many governments have uttered a quiet 'Er, whoops, maybe he was right after all.' Bit late, guys.

OLD, OLD BOYS NETWORK

24

When it comes to distinguished former pupils, Eton is in a class of its own. The archetypal English public school (which first opened its doors today in 1440) has educated a prodigious 19 out of Britain's 47 prime ministers (including David Cameron) and other high-achieving students include George Orwell, Francis Bacon and Ian Fleming. As you might expect, such a top-flight education doesn't come cheap – it currently costs £29,862 a year to attend Eton. Ironically, however, it was actually established by Henry VI as a charity school to provide *free* education to 70 poor boys.

BASEBALL IS KIDS' STUFF

25 John Newbery was a publisher from Berkshire who saw that children's books could be both entertaining and educational. His *A Little Pretty Pocket-Book* (published today in 1744) had rhymes for each letter of the alphabet as well as woodcut illustrations. The book seems simple today, but it was nothing short of revolutionary then, and the very popular book helped establish writing for young people as a literary endeavour. Newbery became known as 'The Father of Children's Literature'. Curiously, his *Pocket-Book* also contains the first printed reference to 'baseball'.

GENE GENIUS

26 Today in 2000, scientists from the Sanger Centre in London handed over the decoded human genome to the world. They had unravelled 85 per cent of the 3 billion DNA base pairs – the blueprint for every aspect of your body, from the capillaries in your lungs to the colour of your eyes. Effectively, all the ingredients that makes you *you*. The Human Genome Project could benefit every human on Earth, and many believe it is modern science's greatest achievement.

THAT KEBAB COST *HOW* MUCH?!

27 Given that English banks are open for about four hours a day, it makes sense that we invented the cash machine. The world's first proper ATM was installed at Barclays Bank in Enfield Town today in 1967, and first used four days later by actor Reg Varney. Today there are 1.7 million worldwide. The pioneering Enfield machine was also the first in the world to be vandalised. One in eight men admit to using a cash machine while being too drunk to remember it. Which explains why nights out seem to cost so much.

COMPUTER SAYS YES

28 Some people are so far ahead of their time it's scary. Charles Babbage was born in London in 1791, but he had the foresight to invent the first practical computer – the Difference Engine. This mechanical number-cruncher would have been 11 feet long, had 8,000 moving parts and weighed 5 tons – if only Victorian engineers had been able to follow his advanced designs. It wasn't until the Science Museum built a replica and turned it on, today in 1991, that they discovered it worked perfectly. It could even print its results!

THE MAGIC BEGINS

29 Harry Potter has thrilled a whole generation of children since he first hit the shelves today in 1997. *Harry Potter and the Philosopher's Stone* was the first novel in the seven-book series, and at first even the publishers only had modest hopes for the tale: they only printed 500 copies, and Gloucestershire-born author J.K. Rowling's advance was just £2,500. But within two years, the book was topping bestseller lists worldwide, with sales well into the hundreds of millions. A new popular legend had been created.

BUT MUMMY, FISH DON'T HAVE HANDS

30 Fish fingers are one of those feel-good foods that we English adore. The first ever fish finger recipe appeared today in 1900 in the *Tamworth Herald*, but they only really took off by accident in 1955. Herring producers tried boosting sales by creating a battered, crumbed oblong called 'herring savouries'. They tried to showcase its tastiness by also producing a bland control product made from cod. But fish fans flipped for the cod, not the herring, and their trade took even more of a battering – by 1965, cod fish fingers made up 10 per cent of the country's entire fish consumption.

JULY

LANDMARK LEGISLATION

Before this day in 1948, the owner of a building could knock it down if they fancied, no matter how beautiful it was. England lost hundreds of historic structures to the whims of landlords and the greed of developers. Then the Town and Country Planning Act was passed, requiring planning permission for new buildings and giving local authorities the power to preserve woodland or buildings of architectural or historic interest. It was an added hurdle for developers, but a blessing for those of us who love our country's beautiful buildings. There are now more than 376,000 listed buildings in England.

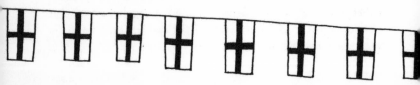

WATERY WONDER

2 When Tsar Nicholas I of Russia told his pal the Duke of Devonshire that he might pop round to Chatsworth for a visit in the new year, the Duke decided to spruce the old place up a bit. His main home improvement was to dig a 9-acre lake high on the moors behind the house, and link this via 2½ miles of conduit to a fountain in the grounds. When this 'Emperor Fountain' was first turned on, today in 1844, it spouted to a hugely impressive 296 feet (90m), making it the tallest in the world. Alas, the Tsar was forced to change his travel plans and never did see the fountain. It's still the highest gravity-fed gusher in the world.

SWEETLY DONE

3 Is there a more English summer experience than tucking into a punnet of delicious strawberries and cream at Wimbledon (and paying £2.50 for the privilege)? Strawberries were once a fruit you enjoyed for just a few weeks every year, being notoriously hard to grow. But then an Isleworth market gardener called Michael Keens spent years selecting, nurturing and developing new varieties of strawberries. Today in 1806 he exhibited the first successful large-fruit cultivar. Almost all popular strawberry varieties are descended from this 'Keens' Seedling'. It's thanks to him that Wimbledon can sell 28,000kg of the fruits during the tournament, doused with 7,000 litres of fresh cream.

LIGHT WHERE YOU LIKE IT

The Anglepoise lamp is still the epitome of the light that is both extremely practical and very stylish, and it was patented today in 1932 by designer George Carwardine, from Bath. He was actually a car designer, and at the time was specialising in vehicle suspension systems – which is where his idea for the Anglepoise's jointed, spring-tensioned design came from. Anglepoise lamps were banned in the BBC in 1948. The head of the variety department thought scriptwriters working under their low, atmospheric light would create 'degenerate' programming ideas.

STREAKING TAKES OFF, 1799

On a normal 18th-century Friday evening in the City of London, a man was arrested as he ran from Cornhill to Cheapside. He was rather out of breath and completely naked. When asked for an explanation by the bewildered constables, he cheerfully admitted it was for a wager of 10 guineas (worth £735 today). And so the modern sensation of streaking was born. In its birthday suit, obviously.

JOHN, THIS IS PAUL

It was a typical summer fete in England in 1957 – there were Scouts and Guides on decorated floats, Morris dancers and the crowning of the Rose Queen. A young band called The Quarrymen played some skiffle songs in a field behind Woolton church. As the local police dog display team followed them on to the stage, the band's 16-year-old lead singer, John, went into the Scout hut. A friend introduced him to 15-year-old Paul, who played John a couple of tunes on his guitar. A few weeks later Paul McCartney was in John Lennon's band and world music got a shot in the arm it would never recover from. Indeed, culture, society and the world at large woke up to a new sound. The Beatles (as they would later call themselves) would go on to sell 1.5 *billion* records and be one of the most popular, and influential, groups of all time.

A LEGEND IN LYCRA

It was a big day for English cycling fans today in 2012 – Bradley 'Wiggo' Wiggins took the yellow jersey in the Tour de France. He didn't relinquish it for the next 15 days, crossing the finish line in Paris to become the first ever English winner of the iconic bike race. Manxman Mark Cavendish won the final stage, and Chris Froome was second overall – he went on to win it himself the following year. Wiggo, of course, took gold the following month in the London Olympics.

CAN YOU DIG IT?

8 Archaeologists now work carefully in teams, according to a strict and careful methodology. But back in the 19th century, if you were rich, determined and English enough, you could just thunder straight on in and start discovering things. Sir Arthur Evans (born today in 1851) exemplified these early Indiana Joneses. He bounded around exotic locations and discovered many remarkable treasures such as the Palace of Knossos on Crete and the entire Minoan civilisation. He was knighted for his discoveries.

WIMBLEDON SERVES UP

9 The Championships, Wimbledon, is the oldest tennis tournament in the world and the most prestigious. It has been held at the All England Club in the London suburb of Wimbledon since this day in 1877 and is the only major championship still played on grass. And quite right too. When Walter Clopton Wingfield, a major in the 66th (Berkshire) Regiment of Foot, invented the game during a party on his estate in 1873, it was on his garden lawn.

Major Walter Clopton Wingfield

SPACE AGE TV

10 Telstar, the first satellite to supply a live transatlantic television feed, and the first privately sponsored space launch, was blasted into orbit today in 1962. Although launched by NASA, it was actually co-designed by the General Post Office in England and internationally co-ordinated from BBC Television Centre in London. It also successfully relayed through space the first telephone calls and fax images.

WHAT A LOO

11 Waterloo Station (opened today in 1848) is one of the world's biggest and busiest stations, with 88 million passengers a year passing through its barriers. That's over 240,000 travellers a day (in case you don't have a calculator to hand). Until 2009, the station even had its own police station, with three cells. It is also the Northern Line underground station for those wishing to visit the extremely popular tourist attraction the London Eye. Its name derives from the scene of a famous military victory, Wellington's final defeat of Napoleon in 1815. It's also the scene of one of the most melancholically English of pop songs, 'Waterloo Sunset' by the Kinks.

NEW TYPE OF NOVEL DETECTED

12 *The Moonstone*, by Wilkie Collins, was published today in 1868 and almost single-handedly launched one of the most popular of all fiction genres: the detective novel. Collins' tale includes several elements that would become staples of this type of story, including a robbery in a country house, a skilled investigator, bungling local plods, red herrings, a 'locked room' murder, a reconstruction of the crime, and a twist in the tail. It also sold absolute bucketloads, spawning many an imitator.

WHO'S WHOM

13 Readers of the *St James's Chronicle* in 1780 would this morning have seen this advertisement: 'John Debrett begs leave most respectfully to acquaint the Nobility and Gentry and his readers in general that he is removed from the late Mr William Davis's the corner of Sackville Street to Mr Almon's Bookseller and Stationer, opposite Burlington House, where he hopes he shall be honoured with their commands.' The ad obviously worked: this is the same Debrett whose name has for more than two centuries adorned *the* reference tome of the English nobility. And if you need to check – no, you aren't in it.

HERE'S LOOKING AT YOU ...

14 Marie Tussaud (born Anna Maria Grosholtz) was French, and she honed her waxwork-making skills by making death masks from the decapitated heads of executed citizens during the French Revolution. Charming lady. But it was in England that she established her world-famous waxwork museum, which took up residence in its well-known building on the Marylebone Road in London today (Bastille Day, appropriately enough) in 1884.

GET YOUR BROLLIES OUT

15 Swithun was a 9th-century Bishop of Winchester who was canonised for miraculously restoring some broken eggs. Wow. Legend says that the weather on his feast day (today) will continue for 40 days. Modern science backs up this old tale: around now the jet stream settles into a pattern that usually holds steady until the end of August. If it lies north of Britain then continental high pressure can move in, otherwise wet Atlantic weather systems take charge.

THE NOT-SO SECRET SERVICE

16 For eighty years, no one had even admitted that one of our country's greatest institutions existed (despite everyone knowing full well that it did). Then, today in 1993, the Secret Service decided to blow its own cover. Stella Rimington became MI5's first Director General to pose for the cameras as she launched a brochure outlining the organisation's activities. When MI5 later began advertising job vacancies, it received 12,000 applications from wannabe Bonds on the first day alone.

THE PERFECT PUNCHLINE

17 It's thanks to *Punch* that today we refer to a humorous illustration as a 'cartoon'. The famous magazine first appeared in London today in 1841 and was hugely influential for most of its life until it faded out in the 1990s. Its gentle, sophisticated English wit was enjoyed by readers from Charlotte Brontë to Queen Victoria, it could boast Charles Dickens as an editor and on its drawing staff were E.H. Shepard (who illustrated *Winnie the Pooh*) and John Tenniel (who illustrated *Alice in Wonderland*).

X MARKS THE VOTE

18 Voting could be a boisterous business before this day in 1872. Landowners virtually ruled their employees, and so could direct their vote, either by standing over them at the ballot or sending an agent to do so. They could also bribe independent voters, many of whom took bungs from both sides. Then the Prime Minister, William Gladstone, introduced secret ballot voting, and although some landowners decried it for being 'unmanly', it ushered in a fairer democratic system.

ENGINEERING EXCELLENCE

19 When it comes to building revolutionary machines, there is one Englishman who stands in particular esteem: Isambard Kingdom Brunel. He built famous bridges (including the Clifton Suspension Bridge), dockyards and the Great Western Railway, for which he designed the viaducts, tunnels, stations and even the locomotives. He constructed the world's first tunnel under a river (the Thames Tunnel), his *Great Britain* was the first steamship driven by a screw propeller, while the *Great Western* (launched today in 1837) was the largest and fastest ship in the world and made the transatlantic voyage in record time.

OLD BOOKS A SPECIALITY

20 In these days of blogging and self-publishing, it's strange to think that in the 16th century you had to get the King's permission to print a book. But today in 1534, Cambridge University was granted letters patent by Henry VIII to do just that. This makes it the world's oldest publishing house. Its authors include the heaviest of the intellectual heavy hitters of the last half-millennium, among them John Milton, William Harvey, Isaac Newton, Bertrand Russell and Stephen Hawking. The Press also has its own shop, which has sold books since at least 1581, making it the oldest known bookshop site in the country.

BIRD-BRAINED

21 Today you can see the very bizarre tradition of 'swan upping' on the River Thames heading to its triumphant finale. Five days ago, men from the Dyers' and Vintners' Companies of the City of London piled into rowing boats and set off from Sunbury. As they went, they caught all the swans they saw, counted them and released them. You might wonder what the point of this is: after all, it's not like the elegant creatures are endangered. Well, we've been doing it since the 12th century, it's an English tradition, and that's all there is to it.

PLIMSOLL'S OUTBURST

22 Bellowing in rage at the Prime Minister is something most of us do in private, but when Samuel Plimsoll did it in Parliament today in 1875, it helped pass a new law that saved thousands of sailors' lives. Bristol-born Plimsoll wanted to stop overloaded ships putting to sea and was angry because his Merchant Shipping Act was being scuttled by ship-owning MPs. Protecting vested interests, the honourable members? Surely not! Anyway, his outburst worked, and the Act was passed. It established, among other safety measures, the mark indicating a ship's loading limit, now known worldwide as the Plimsoll line.

REIGN OF THE SPEED KING

23 Today in 1955, English speed king Donald Campbell set his first world record when he shot across Ullswater in the Lake District in his jet-boat *Bluebird K7* at a tourist-terrifying 202.15mph. The Surrey-born speedster would go on to break more water speed records than anyone else, and become the only person to break the land and water speed records in the same year (1964). Tragically, Campbell died when *Bluebird* crashed during another record attempt in 1967.

PUKKA CHUKKA

24 Modern polo wasn't invented in England (it originated in India), but we certainly popularised it and turned it into the high-society happening it is famous for being today. Cowdray Park in West Sussex is the spiritual home of English polo and the venue for the Gold Cup, the sport's premier trophy. The Park held its first tournament today in 1910.

COFFEE AND CAT FOOD

25 Engineer Christopher Cockerell from Cambridge was experimenting with a coffee tin and a cat food tin, placing one inside the other and blasting air into the gap between them with a hair dryer (as one does), when he discovered something interesting – a high-pressure cushion of air gave the cans unexpected lift. He used this concept to create the modern hovercraft, which made its famous crossing of the Channel today in 1959. The Duke of Edinburgh insisted on taking the wheel when inspecting the invention, and badly dented the craft.

OH, I DO LIKE TO BE A MILE FROM THE SEASIDE

26 Ah, the divebombing seagulls, loudly bleeping amusement arcades, loitering youths, grumpy fishermen and the gentle perfume of old seaweed – what could be more wonderfully English than the pleasure pier? The world's first was built at Ryde, on the Isle of Wight, and opened today in 1814. Early piers were designed to save boat-trippers wading through a mile of mud to shore when the tide was out. But they soon became holiday destinations in themselves, with fairs, theatres and food stalls. Southend-on-Sea pier stretches for 1.34 pleasure-packed miles (2.16km), making it the longest in the world.

THE TORCH LIGHTS UP LONDON - AGAIN

27 When the games of the XXX Olympiad opened on this day in 2012, it was the third time that London had hosted the Summer Olympics (they were also here in 1908 and 1948). No other city has done so. And our athletes didn't just exceed expectations, they smashed them, winning 65 medals – 29 of them golds. Add to that the sensational opening ceremony, amazing stadia and all-round feel-good factor, and London 2012 has to go down as the best £9 billion ever spent.

COMET SENSE

28 If you can hang on until today in 2061, you can watch the return of the comet named after one of England's greatest astronomers, Edmond Halley. He was the first man to work out that comets return regularly: the comet seen in 1682 was the same one that had appeared in 1607 and 1531. He predicted it would return in 1758, but died 16 years before he was proved right. The comet named after him is one of the nippiest things in the solar system, clocking 157,838mph. Halley also stumped up the cash for the publication of Newton's *Principia Mathematica*, one of the most important scientific documents of all time.

LE TUNNEL

29 Admittedly we can only take half the credit, as the French started digging from their end too, but the Channel Tunnel is still an impressive achievement. Margaret Thatcher and François Mitterrand signed the agreement today in 1987, and seven years later the first passengers were travelling '*sous la Manche*'. At 23.5 miles, it has the longest undersea portion of any tunnel in the world and is 31.4 miles long overall. The Eurostar Shuttle trains that carry road freight through the tunnel are the largest railway wagons in the world.

PAPERBACKS BREAK OUT

Readers the world over have been tucking battered paperbacks in their jacket pockets for decades now. But that wasn't possible before today in 1935, when the first Penguin paperback appeared. Costing just sixpence, it put a quality read within everyone's reach, and within a year one million Penguin books had been sold. And, unlike a Kindle, they don't break when you sit on them by mistake.

BULLY FOR YOU

On this day in 1712, a satirist called John Arbuthnot created 'a heroic archetype of the freeborn Englishman' – John Bull. This character was a plain-talking, hard-drinking farmer in a Union Jack waistcoat with a bulldog by his side. Fond of country sports, he was honest, generous, stubborn, had a zest for life and was ready to fight for what he believed in. For some reason, it's an image of an Englishman that has stood the test of time.

AUGUST

HIS HEAD WAS BUBBLING WITH IDEAS

Joseph Priestley from Yorkshire was an intellectual decathlete who wrote hugely influential texts on philosophy, politics, science and religion, among many other topics. He made discoveries regarding electricity, photosynthesis and respiration, and today in 1774 he discovered nothing less than a new type of air – today we know it as oxygen. More importantly, for lovers of cool and relaxing whisky drinks, he invented soda water.

HUDSON FINDS HIS BAY (SORT OF)

2 Henry Hudson was one of the greatest, and most unsung, of all English explorers. Today in 1610 he discovered the huge bay that bears his name. The Hudson River in New York is also named after him, as are Hudson County, the Henry Hudson Bridge, the Hudson Strait, and the town of Hudson, New York. The Hudson's Bay Company got so rich through fur trading that it shaped the present international boundaries of western North America. His obscurity is possibly because he actually thought Hudson Bay was the Pacific Ocean and his crew got so hacked off that they cast him and his son adrift, never to be seen again.

EXPLORING THE COSMIC PLANE

3 Today in 1904, Francis Younghusband trod new ground when he became one of the first Westerners ever to enter the forbidden city of Lhasa. Unfortunately, he was a bit rough with the locals, but Younghusband at least seems to have regretted this, and indeed took on some Eastern karma to make amends. He had a mystical experience which suffused him with 'love for the whole world'. He became a sort of proto-hippy who believed in the power of cosmic rays, and claimed that there are extraterrestrials with translucent flesh on the planet Altair.

BOWLER BORN

4 When William Coke asked his London hatter James Lock to make him a new hat today in 1849, he specified it had to be close-fitting, lower than a top hat and very strong. Coke's uncle was the Earl of Leicester and he wanted a practical hat to protect the heads of the family's gamekeepers. Two hatmakers were commissioned to fulfil the order: Thomas and William Bowler. When Coke came to collect his hat he placed it on the floor and stamped hard on it twice; the hat withstood this test and Coke paid 12 shillings for his 'Bowler'. The hat remains one of the most popular images of Englishness. Curiously, the bowler, not the cowboy hat or sombrero, was the most popular hat in the American West.

WORLD-BEATING BICCIES

5 From humble beginnings as a bakery founded today in 1822 in Reading, Huntley & Palmers became the world's biggest biscuit firm. In 1900 they had 5,000 people making 400 different types of biccie at the world's largest biscuit factory. Huntley & Palmers was probably the first truly global brand; their biscuits travelled the world in decorated tins, symbolising the British Empire in the way that Coca-Cola did for the US. Famous for their high quality, they supplied Scott's ill-fated Antarctic expedition. Indeed, even today, in a hut near the South Pole, his biscuits still await him.

WORLD WIDE WEB CLICKS INTO ACTION

6 The Internet has its origins in the 1960s as a US defence and academic tool. But the World Wide Web was designed to be more open and user-friendly. Anyone with a browser could view webpages containing text, images and videos, and navigate around them using hyperlinks. Basically, it's the more clickable part of the Internet that most of us use every day. And it was thought up by Londoner Tim Berners-Lee, who turned on the web's first client and server today in 1991.

BROOM-BROOM BROOKLANDS

7 There have been many dazzling and superb racing circuits built, but the world's first was Brooklands in Surrey. It held its first ever Grand Prix today in 1926. Unfortunately, the race was won by the French team, but never mind. The legendary banked oval track could house 250,000 spectators and was the preferred venue for many early Land Speed Record attempts.

ARMS AND THE ARMADA

The Spanish Armada of 151 ships aimed to overthrow Elizabeth I. But it met a stalwart and ingenious defence today in 1588 near the port of Gravelines in Flanders. The English Navy used their more manoeuvrable ships and bold tactics (including using fire ships) to rout the Armada and chase it into the North Sea. Severe storms also savaged the Spanish, and only around 67 ships made it back to Spain. No English ships were sunk. The victory marked a lasting shift in world naval balance in England's favour.

BRIGHTON BARES ALL

Today in 1979, Brighton became the first major resort in England to have a nudist beach. Which is notable, considering how flipping freezing our summers tend to be. Frankly, anyone who goes completely nude on our beaches deserves a medal, although working out where to pin it could be tricky.

PROM-TIDDLEY-OM-PROM

10

The 'Last Night of the Proms' might be a little bit *too* English for many people. But the promenade concerts aren't really about flag-waving. When impresario Robert Newman organised the first concert today in 1895, he actually aimed to attract people from all walks of life, particularly those who might not normally appreciate classical music. His proms had low prices and an informal atmosphere. His tradition continues today: the prom season has over 100 concerts in auditoriums and parks across the country, as well as educational and children's events.

NICE ASCOT

11

Royal Ascot is such a glamorous social event that coverage of people's attire far exceeds racing news. The privileged few invited into the Royal Enclosure must obey a strict dress code: morning dress with top hat for gentlemen, while ladies must wear a dress that doesn't reveal too much flesh. But the more fabulous and over-the-top your hat, the better. Over the years, there have been some utterly ridiculous ones, and the event has become a famous English tradition. The first ever Royal Ascot horse race was held on this day in 1711, and now more than 300,000 people come to make a splash during Royal Ascot week.

MORE THAN JUST A MOUTHWASH

12 Today in 1865, 11-year-old James Greenness was admitted to hospital with a compound fracture of his leg. The very high risk of infection in those days made that a potential death sentence. But luckily for James, the doctor treating him was Joseph Lister from Essex, who was about to make a monumental medical breakthrough. Lister wondered if clean hands and instruments and a swab of a 5 per cent carbolic acid solution might help prevent infection. Young James was his guinea pig. The boy made a full recovery and the medical world had antiseptics.

BREARLEY CLEANS UP

13 In 1913, Sheffield metallurgist Harry Brearley was trying to prevent rifle barrels from corroding, and was experimenting by dissolving them in acid. He noticed that steel with a high chromium content didn't dissolve. After researching varying proportions, today Harry produced an alloy with 12.8 per cent chromium, which he called 'rustless steel'. Its name was later changed to 'stainless steel' and a whole new metal industry was born.

BEACH BEAUTIES

14 After the strict morality and decorum of the Victorian era, the Edwardian age brought in a little more daring and frivolity, such as the world's first ever beauty contest, which was held today in 1908 in Folkestone. Despite containing entrants from all over the world, it was a local 18-year-old girl from East Molesey, Nellie Jarman, who swept the judges off their sandy feet. Of course, since the bikini wouldn't be invented for another 38 years, it wasn't *that* daring. But jolly good fun all the same.

TWIST AND SCREAM

15 When The Beatles ran out onto the stage at Shea Stadium, New York, tonight in 1965, it was a moment that changed music history. The attendance of 60,000 was a record, and the gross take was the highest for any show-business performance. It showed that huge outdoor concerts could work, and so stadium rock was born. As for the gig, the noise from the screaming audience was so intense that no one could really hear the music, not even the band. Towards the end of their set John began playing the keyboard with his elbows to see if anyone would notice. They didn't.

SUBTEXT

16 Before today in 1858 it took at least ten days for a message to cross the Atlantic from the US to England. But now it took a matter of minutes thanks to the first transatlantic telegraph, which was inaugurated by Queen Victoria and the then US President, James Buchanan. The system failed after a month and it took seven years to convince sceptical investors to fund the repair. And you thought waiting in all day for BT to come round was bad enough.

LICK IT AND SEE

17 Whatever you think of the Royal Mail now, in the 1830s it was much, much worse. Letters were paid for by the recipient, who had the option to simply refuse delivery, and the more you paid, the further the letter went. Bad news if Granny lived in Berwick-upon-Tweed and you were in Land's End. Then Rowland Hill from Kidderminster had a brilliant idea: low and uniform rates based on weight and the prepayment of postage, receipted with a stamp. It was clearly a winner, and today in 1839 the Postage Act was passed. In May the following year the Penny Black, the world's first adhesive postage stamp, appeared on letters.

OASIS GO SUPERSONIC

18 Oasis were the power behind the Britpop music boom of the 1990s and they played their first ever live gig today in 1991 at the Boardwalk club in Manchester. Noel Gallagher wasn't in the band yet – he was still a roadie for Inspiral Carpets – and he only went to the gig to check out his younger brother's band. He suddenly realised that with the addition of his songs the band could go far. Within a few years they would become one of the most successful English bands of all time, with over 40 million records sold.

READY, STEADY, COE!

19 There was a time when England left the rest of the world standing in middle-distance running. That dominance pretty much started today in 1979, when Sebastian Coe completed an incredible hat-trick. In July he had bagged the 800-metre and mile world records and today he also became the fastest man ever to run the 1500 metres. With the Steves Ovett and Cram hot on his heels, golden days were ahead for English athletics.

DARWIN CHANGES THE WORLD

20 As ideas go, Charles Darwin's concept of adaptation by natural selection has to be one of the most important and far-reaching that anyone has ever had. The theory that would later become *On the Origin of Species* was first published today in 1858, and, although derided (and considered controversial) by many people, this work is now the cornerstone of modern evolutionary understanding. Since the theory has become embraced widely (though not universally just yet) the world will look back at Darwin's achievements as the day all life on Earth started to understand where it came from.

NO LADDER IN HER TIGHTS

21 Today in 1976, Mary Langdon of Sussex became the first ever English firewoman. That might seem like a slow response to changing times, but our country is actually one of the most progressive countries when it comes to emergency equality. We now have more than 200 full-time women firefighters, and another 200 serving as retained firefighters.

CAMRA'S FIRST AGM... APPARENTLY

22 Holding a tasty pint of real ale in your hand – as opposed to fizzy European lager or weak American beer – is one of those magical feelings that is a truly English tradition. Real ale usually looks like thick muddy water, and is often called ridiculous names like Piston Bitter, Bishop's Finger and Old Speckled Hen, but also has a depth of flavour that always warms the cockles. And this proper ale-drinking tradition is set to continue long into the future thanks to Bill Mellor, Graham Lees, Michael Hardman and Jim Makin, who held CAMRA's (Campaign for Real Ale) first AGM today in 1972 at the Rose Inn, Nuneaton. Although details of this first meeting are a little hazy...

THE PRANK THAT'S OUT OF THIS WORLD

23 Doug Bower and his pal Dave Chorley were having a few ales today in 1976 in a Hampshire boozer when they hatched a grand plan to put England on the UFO-hotspot map. Getting together some planks, rope and hats with wire sights dangling from the brim, they flattened out a perfectly neat ring in a field of corn – the world's first artificial crop circle. Newspapers wrote it off as a natural phenomenon, so Doug and Dave upped the ante, creating ever more intricate designs. Now it was clearly aliens.

A CORKER OF AN IDEA

24 Being an inventive nation is something to celebrate, particularly when what we've come up with is a better way to open wine bottles. And today in 1795, Samuel Henshall from Oxford was awarded patent number 2061 for his improved corkscrew. This revolutionary design used a button between the shank and the worm to free the cork and make it pull more smoothly. So drinkers could now get to the wine faster and without finding any corky bits in it. Cheers, Samuel!

NICE DAY FOR A DIP

25 The English Channel is the busiest stretch of water in the world, but that hasn't stopped people wanting to swim across it. The 21-mile gap across the Strait of Dover is wide enough to be a huge physical challenge, while narrow enough to be physically possible. The first person to achieve the feat was Captain Matthew Webb, from Dawley in Shropshire, who hauled himself out onto a French beach on this day in 1875. His crossing took 21 hours and 45 minutes. The current record for the blue-chip event is 6 hours 55 minutes, set by Australian Trent Grimsey in 2012.

LONGBOWS BECOME LEGENDARY

26 The military supremacy of the English longbow was established on this day in 1346 at the Battle of Crécy. The French had a huge force of up to 100,000 men against the English and Welsh army of 15,000, but they placed too much strategic importance on their armoured knights and crossbowmen. The longbowmen could fire faster and more accurately, and when the knights became literally bogged down, the French were vanquished. Huzzah!

A QUICK WAR BEFORE BREAKFAST

27 If you're going to have a war, best make it a quick one. And today in 1896 saw us win the world's shortest ever conflict – the Anglo–Zanzibar War. This fracas lasted approximately 38 minutes, from 9.02 a.m. – when our gunships opened fire on the Sultan of Zanzibar's palace – to 9.40 a.m., when he decided it was probably a jolly good idea to surrender.

CARNIVAL CHRISTENED

28 Nowadays up to 2 million people throng London's Notting Hill for the largest street carnival in Europe. But today in 1964 less than 100 enjoyed the inaugural party. It started when a group of Trinidadian immigrants decided to throw an impromptu carnival procession through their neighbourhood, complete with steel band. The spectacle caught the English public eye and the seeds of the current Carnival were sown.

CHARGED WITH BRILLIANCE

29 Michael Faraday was a humble blacksmith's son from Surrey who happened to be a scientific genius. Today in 1831 he discovered electromagnetic induction – how a change in magnetic intensity can produce an electric current. Soon after, he discovered that electricity was generated when a magnet passed through a helix wound with wire. He thus invented the transformer and dynamo, key elements of the electric motor. It was largely thanks to Faraday that electricity could be put to practical use. He is easily one of the most influential scientists in history.

SUCCESS IS IN THE BAG

30 Sometimes being English sucks. And that couldn't be any truer for Hubert Cecil Booth from Gloucester, who today in 1901 patented the first powered vacuum cleaner. Booth got his big break, and recognition, when his machine was used to clean the carpets of Westminster Abbey before Edward VII's coronation. But his device was so large it had to be pulled from house to house *by a horse*. Obviously, that was never going to be a popular household product, so when an American upstart called Hoover built a smaller machine he…well, cleaned up.

NO FERTILISER REQUIRED

31

Sheep poo was an essential addition to almost every fine English lawn before today in 1830 – the only way to cut the grass was with hungry herbivores or gangs of men with scythes. Then Edwin Budding from Gloucestershire patented the first mechanical lawnmower. This device would go on to revolutionise Victorian recreational life – the garden party and horticulture itself became hugely popular. So, too, did sports such as croquet, golf and football, which could now be played on a decent grass surface. No longer would a player's triumphant winning shot come to a sticky end...

SEPTEMBER

IT'S BAD FOR YOU, YOU KNOW

It seems obvious now, but before this day in 1950, people had no concrete evidence that smoking was linked to lung cancer and heart disease. In fact, tobacco companies often highlighted their products' health *benefits*. Then physiologist Richard Doll (with Austin Hill) studied lung cancer patients in 20 London hospitals and discovered that smoking was the only factor they had in common. Doll stopped smoking himself, and today published his findings in the *British Medical Journal*.

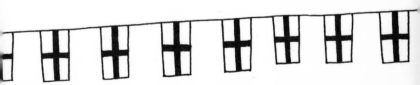

POUR ON WATER

2 The Great Fire of London, which started today in 1666, was tragic for the city's displaced inhabitants but it was probably a good thing for England in the long run. London had been a filthy, overcrowded warren of a capital; the fire incinerated many slums and all traces of the previous year's plague, and the devastation allowed the capital to be rebuilt in brick and stone, not wood. The new streets were wider and cleaner, and many beautiful new public buildings were created, including the majestic new St Paul's Cathedral.

HIS UNTIDINESS SAVED HUMANITY

3 Don't you hate it when you come back from holiday to find the place in a mess? Biologist Alexander Fleming certainly did when he returned to his laboratory in St Mary's Hospital, London, today in 1928 – there were contaminated bacteria cultures all over his workbench. Luckily, though, while he was away a fungus had killed patches of bacteria. Fleming was amazed, and he soon developed that fungus into penicillin, the most efficacious life-saving drug in the world. It would conquer syphilis, gangrene and tuberculosis, among many other infections, saving an estimated 200 million lives to date.

THE MODS ARE HERE

4

With their sharp suits, Italian scooters and distinctive hairstyles and music tastes, Mods were a major part of British youth culture in the 50s, 60s and 70s. 'Mods' came from 'modernists', reflecting the group's origins among young fans of 'modern' jazz. The term encompassed a whole subculture, but the movement was first brought to a wider audience in London writer Colin MacInnes' cult novel *Absolute Beginners*, which was published today in 1959.

A NEW CHAPTER IN BOOKSHOP HISTORY

5

Next time you pick up a Brontë or Dickens novel at the station, you can feel proud that your purchase is possible thanks to William Henry Smith from London. He introduced the world's first railway bookstall, at Euston in 1848. It proved rather popular, and the company became the world's first chain store, WH Smith. The company has managed many other innovations, including creating the ISBN book catalogue system in 1966. And William Smith Jnr was the first person to publish (today in 1856) the claim that Francis Bacon was the author of Shakespeare's plays.

TANKS FOR THE MEMORIES

6 A new era in military history dawned on this day in 1915, when the first ever tank rolled off the production line of the Wellington Foundry in Lincoln. Weighing 16.5 tonnes, it was 26 feet long, had a scorching top speed of 2mph and was nicknamed 'Little Willie' after the press's mocking term for the German Imperial Crown Prince Wilhelm.

GRACE OUR DARLING

7 Some English heroes are so brave it takes your breath away. Grace Darling was the daughter of a lighthouse keeper from Bamburgh, Northumberland. A savage storm forced the steamship *Forfarshire* aground today in 1838 and broke the vessel up, stranding nine people on a rock offshore amid giant waves. Twenty-two-year-old Grace calmly got into a boat with her father and rowed over a mile through mountainous seas to rescue the sailors and, in the process, become a national heroine. Modest as well as courageous, Grace preferred the quiet life with her family to the limelight.

DR SNOW BRAVES CHOLERA
TO SAVE THOUSANDS

8 In 1854 cholera outbreaks killed thousands in England's cities. People thought the disease spread by 'bad air' and did little to halt its progress. Dr John Snow of York thought differently, and went to the streets of Soho to investigate. By carefully mapping the cases he discovered that a water pump in Broad Street was the centre of the outbreak. A cesspit had contaminated the well. Today he begged authorities to intervene by the simple action of removing the pump's handle; they were sceptical, but did so. The outbreak faded away. Snow's work was one of the biggest events in the history of public health and helped to found the science of epidemiology.

THE FLYING POSTIE

9 England notched up another pioneering achievement today in 1911, when the world's first scheduled airmail post service took off. It may only have linked the London suburb of Hendon with Windsor in Berkshire, but that wasn't bad for 1911, less than eight years after the invention of powered flight.

THE 'COUGHING MAJOR' CLEANS UP

10 When Major Charles Ingram won the top prize on *Who Wants To Be A Millionaire?* today in 2001, some ne'er-do-wells had the temerity to suggest that his chum in the audience, Tecwen Whittock, had signalled the correct answers to him by coughing. As if one of Her Majesty's upstanding officers would possibly ever cheat at anything! Poppycock! No, today we celebrate Major Ingram's brains, bravado and initiative and say, 'Jolly well done, old man!'

GOOD NEWS FOR PANDAS

11 Today in 1961 the World Wildlife Fund opened its doors to our furred and feathered friends. Founded by English biologist Julian Huxley and environmentalist Max Nicholson, the WWF (renamed the World Wide Fund for Nature in 1986) is now the world's largest independent conservation organisation with over 5 million supporters worldwide. It funds around 1,300 conservation and environmental projects, making a lot of happy pandas.

GETTING THE POINT

12 Cleopatra's Needle may be one of London's best-loved monuments, but it's also the most badly named. Erected on the Thames Embankment today in 1878, the 68-foot, 224-ton red granite obelisk was gifted to us by Egypt to commemorate victories at the Battle of the Nile in 1798 and the Battle of Alexandria in 1801. But the obelisk is almost 3,500 years old, meaning it was already ancient by the time Queen Cleopatra VII came to the throne.

BESSEMER FORGES AHEAD

13 Iron is strong but brittle. By the 1850s, several iron bridges had collapsed with disastrous consequences, and engineers longed to be able to use steel. This is more malleable, but it was also then very expensive. Sir Henry Bessemer, after years of experimentation, today in 1856 published details of his eponymous steel-making process in *The Times*. It created the cheaper steel that fuelled a worldwide wave of train- and shipbuilding and made Bessemer very rich indeed.

HANDEL TURNS IT ON

14

Today in 1741, after just 24 days of inspired composing, George Frideric Handel finished his *Messiah*, a monumental musical masterpiece. Living in London and by then a naturalised citizen of these shores, Handel wrote the work in English. It is one of the world's most popular oratorios and its 'Hallelujah' chorus is a particular Christmas favourite.

HARRY IS FINGERED

15

When Harry Jackson stole a set of billiard balls from a house in Denmark Hill, London, he could hardly have thought that he would go down in history. But Jackson made the mistake of stealing the balls from a house that had just been painted, so leaving a fingerprint on a windowsill, just as Scotland Yard was perfecting its fingerprint detection procedures. Harry became the first person in the world to be convicted from fingerprint evidence, and today in 1902 he started seven years in prison. Crime fighters – and crime writers – had a handy new weapon.

THE *MAYFLOWER* SETS SAIL

16 In 1620 King James I was making life uncomfortable for people of non-conformist religions. On this day 102 men, women and children, many of whom were Puritans, sailed from Plymouth aboard the *Mayflower*, seeking a freer life in the New World. After 65 gruelling days at sea they landed at what is now called Plymouth Rock in Massachusetts. The 'Pilgrim Fathers' became the first permanent European settlers in America and helped shape the future United States.

WATER WAY TO GO, NORMAN

England is stuffed with eccentrics, but very few are actually world-beaters. Step forward Norman Buckley, who today in 1956 broke the one-hour world water speed record in his motorboat, *Miss Windermere III*. Norman was remarkable because he was actually a 48-year-old solicitor from Manchester who only designed, built and raced his all-conquering hydrofoil in his spare time.

CORNY, BUT TRUE

The Corn Laws were a 19th-century price-fixing scam – the big market players made money at the expense of everyone else. It wasn't fair, but it was just the way things were done (and still are, some would say). Then Richard Cobden and John Bright formed the Anti-Corn Law League today in Manchester in 1838. They achieved their titular goals eight years later, helping to establish a fully free-trade economy and boosting international trade. It also meant that ordinary people paid less for a loaf of bread. Maybe we could do something similar with the energy companies...

'IT'S NOT FOR GAMES ...'

19

Clive Sinclair from Surrey founded his revolutionary electronics company today in 1973, and within a few short years he put Britain at the forefront of home computing. His ZX80, brought out in 1980, had a tiny 1KB of memory (it would take a million of them to match today's average laptop), but cost just £99.95, bringing it within reach of the average household for the first time. Two years later, Sinclair launched the ZX Spectrum; kids persuaded their parents they needed one for school, it became Britain's best-selling computer and a whole generation of brilliant boffins was born.

TOO POSH TO WASH

20

Every efficiency counted back in the dark wartime days of 1942, and today every household was asked to bathe in no more than 5 inches of water to conserve fuel. This might have kicked up a dirty old ruckus, had not the Royal Family instantly announced that they had painted black lines on the baths in every palace in England to keep water levels low, no matter how mucky the monarchy got.

TA, MAC!

21 Next time you're stuck in a 12-mile tailback on the M25, don't despair – take pride! The road you are not moving very fast on only exists thanks to the work of pioneering engineer John McAdam. Born today in 1756, he revolutionised road construction the world over by using a new process to rebuild the Bristol turnpike. Starting with a firm base of large stones, he packed crushed stone bound with gravel on top and formed a camber to ensure rainwater rapidly drained off rather than seeping into the road's foundations. It was the biggest step forward in road-building since the Romans. Later, tar was added to bind the surface's stones together and create an even smoother, harder road – the word 'tarmac' comes from 'tar Macadam'.

FIRST, CATCH YOUR HARE

22 Forget Nigella and Delia, the original English domestic goddess was 23-year-old Mrs Isabella Beeton. Her recipes began appearing in *The Englishwoman's Domestic Magazine* today in 1859, and were a sensation. Beeton's innovations included a list of ingredients at the start of recipes and illustrations so you could see how badly you'd gone wrong. Two years later they were collected as her famous *Book of Household Management*, which became the authority on all things domestic and culinary, even if it did recommend boiling carrots for two hours.

ROW, ROW, ROW YOUR BOAT

23 Today in 2000, Buckinghamshire-born Steve Redgrave won gold at his fifth consecutive Olympic Games. With him in his coxless four were Matthew Pinsent (winning gold at his third consecutive Games), Tim Foster and James Cracknell. The men were cheered on by 22,000 excited spectators as they pipped the Italians into second place by just 0.38 seconds. Redgrave was knighted the next year and has a fair claim to be our greatest Olympian.

MAKING BACON

24 Forget *Blind Date* or *Mr & Mrs* – the oldest relationship game in the world is the Dunmow Flitch, held in the Essex town of Great Dunmow every four years. Dating back to this day in 1104, and mentioned in *The Canterbury Tales*, it's the oldest competition in England. The prize is a 'flitch' of bacon – basically a side of pork. Couples have to persuade a jury that for a year and a day they have 'never once, sleeping or waking, regretted our marriage or wished ourselves single again'. So it's the world's earliest lying competition, then.

GREEN FOR GO

25 No one flies the flag faster than Wing Commander Andy Green, who today in 1997 clocked an incredible 714.144mph (1149,30km/h) in his jet-powered car, *ThrustSSC*. He later raised this record to 763.035mph, becoming the first man to break the sound barrier on land. He is currently planning to break the 1,000mph mark in the rocket-powered car *Bloodhound SSC*.

HAIR RAISING

26 Today in 1968 the country welcomed the dawn of a new era of cultural freedom with the abolition of theatre censorship. The new Theatres Act ended the Lord Chamberlain's powers of censorship, which dated back to 1737. The very next day, the hippy musical *Hair*, which featured nudity and drug-taking, opened in London. The countercultural revolution of the late 1960s had broken down another barrier, never to be put up again.

DO THE LOCOMOTION

If it's ever taken you three hours to travel 20-odd miles by train, don't despair – you're part of a great English tradition. Today in 1825, the world's first passenger railway service rolled into history when George Stephenson's steam engine *Locomotion* pulled passengers the 26 miles from Shildon to Stockton via Darlington in just under three hours. This event sparked a railway boom, and within 50 years there were 160,000 miles of railways around the world.

RADIO GA-GA

It may seem strange today, but there's a whole generation of English folk for whom the two-week festive *Radio Times* was the most exciting publication of the year. The *Radio Times* first appeared today in 1923, and was launched by the BBC because no newspapers would carry radio listings – they feared that increased listenership would decrease their sales. At one time it was the biggest-selling magazine in Europe.

NATIONAL ROAST DINNER DAY

29 Many of us set aside one day a week, never mind once a year, to enjoy a roast dinner with all the trimmings. A joint of tender meat accompanied by roast potatoes, stuffing, vegetables, Yorkshire puddings and home-made gravy makes the home smell of, well, home. Having a national day of roast dinner eating can only be a good thing. Roast dinners are enjoyed around the world, though notably less so in France – hence the French insult for English people is 'les rosbifs' – the roast beefs. To us, it's not an insult – in fact, it's a compliment!

CURRYING FAVOUR WITH THE KING

30 The curry house is one of the world's favourite restaurant experiences, and the first outside the Indian subcontinent opened on this day in London in 1810. The Hindoostanee Coffee House was the dream of Indian traveller and entrepreneur Sake Dean Mahomed. Unfortunately, our genteel classes weren't ready for rogan josh, and the venture soon closed. But Mahomed had another Indian ace up his sleeve, and promptly introduced England to 'shampooing' – a form of aromatherapy. This was massively successful and he was even appointed shampooing surgeon to King George IV.

OCTOBER

THIS ONE STARTS OFF A LITTLE QUIET ...

Is there another DJ who gave more cool bands their big break than John Peel? The Wirral-born muso first broadcast his Radio 1 show today in 1967 and would continue as a presenter on the station for another 37 years. Famous for his extremely eclectic taste, he would think nothing of playing bands as diverse as the Clash, Captain Beefheart and Elmore James in the same half-hour. He was one of the first DJs anywhere to play psychedelic and progressive rock records. Curiously, he was also present at the arraignment of Lee Harvey Oswald in Dallas in 1963, the night before JFK's assassin was himself killed. Peel had passed himself off as a reporter for the *Liverpool Echo*. All that is written on Peel's headstone besides his name is the line 'Teenage dreams, so hard to beat' from his favourite song, 'Teenage Kicks' by the Undertones.

ONE CHANNEL AND NOT MUCH ON

2 A cynic might say that the very first image seen on TV (today in 1925) set the tone for the vast majority of subsequent programming: it was the head of a ventriloquist's dummy. Television's inventor, John Logie Baird, had been born in Scotland, but he made all his major televisual breakthroughs after he moved to the south of England. He built the world's first working television while living in Hastings, using a tea chest, a hatbox, a pair of scissors, some darning needles, some bicycle light lenses, sealing wax and glue. Baird set up his workshop in Soho, where he later invented colour TV, and he gave the first public demonstration of TV in Selfridges department store in London. The world of home entertainment – indeed, the world itself – would never be the same again.

INTERCITY 125 ROLLS OUT

3 It's difficult to imagine when you've been stuck outside York for two hours, but the InterCity 125 train is actually one of our country's great successes. The first one left Paddington for Bristol Temple Meads today in 1976 and, amazingly, arrived three minutes early. The world's fastest diesel train still covers 1,000 miles a day, 7 days a week. Its unique shape is thanks to designer Kenneth Grange from London, who created two other English icons: the Kenwood Chef and the parking meter.

ATLANTIC CROSSING

It might seem strange now with the dominance of Boeing, but England was a pioneer in the jet airliner industry – the first ever transatlantic jet passenger service was launched today in 1958 by Heathrow-based BOAC. Passengers could hop between New York and London on the new de Havilland Comet in the record time of 6 hours and 12 minutes.

WAKLEY HEALS THE WORLD

For nearly two centuries *The Lancet* has been at the cutting edge of medical knowledge (literally – a lancet is a double-edged scalpel).

It was first published today in 1823 by Thomas Wakley, an English surgeon and firebrand reformer. Wakley hated 'quackery' and as well as establishing the world's first peer-reviewed medical journal, he became a radical MP who campaigned fearlessly against the evils of incompetence, privilege and nepotism.

WHOHASN'TDUNITBYNOW?

6 *The Mousetrap* has now reached the point where the very fact that it is an English institution will draw the tourists and so ensure its continued survival, regardless of any inherent quality. Agatha Christie's murder mystery with a shocking twist ending was first performed today in 1952. It has now clocked up more than 25,000 performances and is still running at the St Martin's Theatre, giving it the longest initial run of any play in history. Christie, not anticipating its success, gave the rights of the play to her grandson as a birthday present.

IT PAYS TO COPY

7 Before this day in 1806, if you wanted to copy a document you had to write it out again by hand. Then English inventor Ralph Wedgwood patented carbon paper, one of the most useful office products ever invented. He was financed with a £200 loan from his cousin Josiah Wedgwood (of pottery fame), and in just seven years he had turned this sum into £10,000 in profits. Though you don't see it around so much these days.

WHAT TOWER?

When the Post Office Tower opened today in 1965 it was the tallest building in the country. But because its main purpose was to carry telecommunications traffic, some of which might be sensitive, the tower was officially a secret, and did not appear on Ordnance Survey maps until the 1990s. This despite being 581 feet tall and built in Central London – only in eccentric old England.

CHEERS CHURCHILL

Tipplers on a tight budget can today be proud of Winston Churchill. Our famously strong leader was on a state visit to Denmark in 1950 when Carlsberg presented him with an equally formidable new beer in his honour – Special Brew. Churchill enjoyed his 9 per cent ABV loopy juice so much he sent a thank-you letter and had two crates of it delivered to his London home. It has been fuelling English gentlemen of the road ever since.

IT ALL ADDS UP

10 English eggheads got us into the history books again today in 1961, when their latest creation, the world's first all-electronic desktop calculator, made its debut at the Hamburg Business Equipment Fair. The Bell Punch/Sumlock Comptometer ANITA (A New Inspiration to Arithmetic/Accounting) may not have had a snappy name, but sales were rapid and ANITA heralded a new era of portable calculating devices that meant no one ever had to work out a mind-bendingly difficult sum in their head again.

'YOU COULD BE RIGHT – COME BACK IN 50 YEARS'

11 The world watched in wonder in 2012 when scientists announced they had found the most sought-after thing in the world. No, not a taxi at Victoria station – the Higgs boson. This miraculous morsel of matter creates an invisible energy field that gives everything, from planets to portions of chips, their mass. Its existence was first proposed by Peter Higgs, a physicist from Newcastle upon Tyne, in 1964. He was in the room 48 years later when experiments caught up with his thinking and proved him right. And today in 2013 he was paraded as the latest winner of the Nobel Prize in physics.

I COMPUTE THEREFORE I AM

Alan Turing was a brilliant English mathematician and computer science pioneer, known as the 'father of artificial intelligence'. He spent World War Two cracking German cipher codes and then moved on to computing, developing the idea of the algorithm and computation and paving the way for modern computers. Today in 1950, he published a famous paper on artificial intelligence in which he proposed what has become known as the Turing test: if a machine can answer questions so well that a questioner cannot tell it is not human, then it can be said to have intelligence. No machine has passed the Turing test. Yet...

SOFT HEART, HARD STARE

Visitors sometimes wonder why a major London station is named after a bear, but please don't tell them it's the other way round. The delightful confusion commenced today in 1958 when Paddington Bear made his literary debut. Author Michael Bond found a real bear (well, a real toy) all on its own in a shop by Paddington station and took the lonely fellow home. The eponymous bear is now one of the best-loved characters in children's literature and is singlepawedly responsible for the popularity of marmalade sandwiches. Perhaps we should start a campaign to rename King's Cross 'Pooh Station'.

BATTLE OF HASTINGS

Today in 1066 the English army was routed at the Battle of Hastings and King Harold II killed. A bit of a downer if you were English at the time, but from a long-term perspective it goes down as one of the most formative moments in our history. The Normans changed the language, raised new buildings and reformed the church, bringing a European rather than a Scandinavian influence to bear on English society. It helped us become the lovely, cultured people we English are today...

IT PACKED A PUNCH, ALL RIGHT

Getting your party guests discreetly laced on lethal punch is a grand English tradition. And no one has done it in quite as much style as Admiral Edward Russell, today in 1694. Rather than a punchbowl, Russell used a large marble fountain, adding 200 gallons of brandy, 100 gallons of Malaga wine, 20 gallons of lime juice, 2,500 lemons, half a ton of sugar, 5lb of grated nutmegs,

300 toasted biscuits, and 400 gallons of water. A cabin boy rowed around the punch in a small boat, filling guests' cups. The party continued until the fountain had been drunk dry, a week later.

BRONTË BRILLIANCE

16 The Brontë sisters, from Yorkshire, created some of the most brilliant and best-loved tales in world literature. They suffered universal rejection before Charlotte's *Jane Eyre* was published today in 1847, with Emily's *Wuthering Heights* and Anne's *Agnes Grey* following soon after. Released under male pseudonyms, the books became instant bestsellers. Sadly, all three sisters died early, none of them reaching the age of forty.

ATOMIC ADVANCES

17 If a new generation of nuclear power helps us create a greener future, England will certainly have done its bit. Calder Hall at Sellafield (formerly called Windscale), which opened today in 1956, was the first commercial nuclear power station in the world. It grew out of a project to make atomic bombs, which thankfully we're doing less of these days, and successfully produced electricity for 47 years until decommissioned in 2003.

OCTOBER

GURN AND BEAR IT

England is a bastion of silly traditions. And today's Egremont Crab Fair in Cumbria was established way back in 1267, making it one of the oldest days of fun in the world. Among its many silly harvest festivities is the World Gurning Championships. Simply stick your head through a horse collar, pull the ugliest face you can and you too could go down in history.

MAKE THEE MIGHTIER YET

Edward Elgar's 'Pomp and Circumstance March' is the tune that's guaranteed to bring proud Englishmen and women to their feet, and it was first played by the Liverpool Orchestral Society today in 1901. It was later given words and turned into the song 'Land of Hope and Glory', which is a regular feature of the Last Night of the Proms. The first time it featured at a Promenade concert the audience apparently 'rose and yelled'. It was 'the one and only time in the history of the Promenade concerts that an orchestral item was accorded a double encore'.

LORD OF ALL PUBLISHING

Authors often create new worlds, but few do it on the scale of English writer J.R.R. Tolkien. The final volume of his *The Lord of the Rings* was published today in 1955, and the world went daft for dwarves and hobbits. The book went on to become the second-best-selling novel ever written, shifting over 150 million copies. (In case you're interested, the best-selling, at over 200 million copies, is *A Tale of Two Cities* by another Englishman, Charles Dickens.)

A SOLID PIECE OF THINKING

The modern world would look very different if it weren't for concrete. Admittedly, there would be a few less architectural carbuncles, but there would also be more unstable buildings, wobbly bridges and uneven roads. One of the vital ingredients in concrete is Portland cement, which a Leeds bricklayer called Joseph Aspdin patented today in 1824. He ground and burned clay and limestone to create a material that hardens when mixed with water, naming it after the stone quarried from Portland, Dorset.

ROUTEMASTER ROLLS OUT

22 The red Routemaster bus is one of the most recognisable symbols of England. And the double-deckers with the open platform became an icon for a good reason: they were extremely well made. The Routemaster made its first appearance at the Earl's Court Motor Show today in 1954, and many were still winding their picturesque way through the capital's streets almost half a century later. It wasn't until December 2005 that the last full service finished, with the very last bus being a number 159 from Marble Arch to Streatham.

IVE A GREAT IDEA

23 Apple is, of course, an American computer company, but it owes a large part of its recent success to a chap from Chingford. Sir Jonathan Ive is the brilliant designer who was tasked with engineering a hard drive that could store an entire record collection yet be small enough to carry everywhere (and also very cool to look at). He rose to the challenge and created the revolutionary iPod, which first appeared today in 2001. He also designed the iMac, iPhone and iPad, among other techno-winners.

DRESSED TO KILL

24 Today in 1854, Lord Cardigan was preparing on the eve of what would become one of the most famous events in military history – the Charge of the Light Brigade. Often thought of as the epitome of foolhardy English courage, it also deserves its place in our sartorial history. Cardigan was probably buttoning up the knitted garment that now bears his name. The ill-fated charge itself was part of the Battle of Balaclava, after which the woollen head covering was christened. The overall commander was Lord Raglan, who gave his name to the style of sleeve that runs right over the shoulder. And Raglan fought at Waterloo under Arthur Wellesley, Duke of Wellington and creator of the famous boot.

FOOTBALL KICKS OFF

25 Today in 1863, 13 football clubs met in London to standardise the laws of the game that would rule the world – association football. The game was very different then – you could legally hack a player to the ground with a sharp kick to the shins if you wanted to. Although rolling around like a big girl's blouse afterwards was very much frowned upon.

NO ONE KNOWS WHO THEY WERE ...

26 Stonehenge in Wiltshire is one of the world's great monuments – and mysteries. Dating perhaps from as much as 5,000 years ago, the site has giant sarsen stones in its outer circle that weigh up to 50 tons and were brought from 20 miles away, while the 80 bluestones of the inner circle made a 240-mile trip from the Preseli Mountains in Wales. Today in 1918 Cecil Chubb, the site's owner, passed the 5,000-year-old monument into the nation's care. A good job too – Victorian tourists armed with hammers used to chip off souvenir chunks of the irreplaceable megaliths.

Wish you were here!

44

Stonehenge

LAUNCHED ON A SEA OF COFFEE

27 Who knows where your coffee-shop chatter could lead? In 1688, coffee shops were all the rage (funny how fashions come round again...) and when Edward Lloyd opened his establishment on Tower Street in London on this day, ye olde grande latte was the hippest drink in town. Lloyd's Coffee House became a popular haunt of weary seafarers, who the proprietor supplied with the latest shipping news. Shipowners and agents then began coming to Lloyd's to discuss insurance deals. This led to the founding of the world-famous insurance market Lloyd's of London, as well as Lloyd's Register of Shipping.

TWINKLE TWINKLE LITTLE SATELLITE

28 Somerset-born Arthur C. Clarke was a writer of epic science-fiction tales, including *2001: A Space Odyssey*. He also created spectacular science fact when today in 1945 he predicted the existence of the geostationary orbit. This is the belt 22,000 miles above the equator where a satellite will orbit at the same rate as the earth rotates, essentially 'fixing' it above one spot on the ground and allowing more efficient global communication. In 1974 he also accurately predicted the arrival of the home computer, and with it online banking and shopping.

OCTOBER

SENSE AND SELF-PUBLISHING

29 Jane Austen isn't just one of the most widely read writers in English literature, she practically created the genre of wry romantic fiction. Her classic books are almost constantly being filmed or adapted into modern settings, and they epitomise the quality English costume drama. *Sense and Sensibility* was her first novel to be published, appearing today in 1811. Like many writers of the time, she had to pay the printer for the privilege.

THE RISE OF THE HEMLINE

30 Some people might think the English are a stuffy, uptight bunch. And maybe we are. But that makes it all the more amazing when one does decide to shake one's booty. Today in 1965 was one such moment, when British model Jean Shrimpton wore a very, very short dress to the Melbourne Cup Carnival and caused a sensation. Soon Mary Quant had perfected the miniskirt and 'Swinging London' was leading the world in both fashion and pop culture.

ALLANTIDE

Modern Hallowe'en activities have largely come to us from America, so it's nice that some ancient English traditions have seen a resurgence. One such is Allantide, which has been celebrated in Cornwall on this day for centuries. Children enjoy scoffing large, highly polished 'Allan apples' and young girls throw walnuts in the fire to determine the fidelity of their future husband. Don't ask how they work it out, I'm not sure. It sounds weird and is slightly eccentric, but it's good English fun, and is surely a better tradition for community peace than 'egging' your neighbour's house.

NOVEMBER

PUFFIN POST

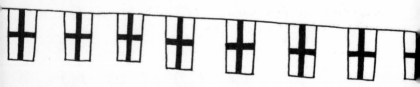

England beats the world when it comes to eccentrics, a fine example being Martin Harman, who bought the island of Lundy in the Bristol Channel in 1924 and promptly proclaimed himself king. Despite being monarch of just a few dozen people and several thousand seabirds, he had to do things properly, so today in 1929 he issued Lundy's very own set of postage stamps. Their value was in 'Puffins'.

MOTORING INTO THE FUTURE

2 When England got its first full-length motorway with the opening of the M1 today in 1959, it promised a brave new age of driving pleasure. There was no speed limit, no central barrier and, with only 13,000 vehicles a day using the road (rather than today's 88,000), it was probably a jolly pleasant way to get from Watford to Rugby. How times change…

THE PEERLESS SNACK

3 Had no one else in the world ever thought of putting a bit of ham in between two slices of bread before the Fourth Earl of Sandwich? Perhaps, with him being an earl rather than a prole, people tended to notice when he did something interesting. His delicious invention came about when the gambling-mad peer couldn't bear to leave the card table and ordered some meat tucked between two pieces of bread brought to him. His chums then requested 'the same as Sandwich'. Today is widely celebrated as National Sandwich Day, so get your pickle out. Mind you, it's good that the snack was named after his title, rather than his surname – then you'd be having a cheese and ham Montagu for your lunch.

NATURALLY THE BEST

4

Pulsars, plate tectonics, the ozone hole, nuclear fission, the structure of DNA, cloning and the human genome sequence all have one thing in common – the world first heard about these scientific breakthroughs in the pages of *Nature*. First published on this day in 1869, in London, it's the world's most cited scientific publication, and getting your research paper into it is a big, big deal. The journal's name came from a line by famous English Romantic poet William Wordsworth: 'To the solid ground of nature trusts the Mind that builds for aye.'

THE FALL GUY

5

Guy Fawkes Night is one of the defining days in our national calendar, when we light bonfires and let off fireworks to celebrate the defeat of the Gunpowder Plot of 1605. Fawkes' attempt to blow up King James I was betrayed and he was caught red-handed with barrels of gunpowder in a cellar under the House of Lords. Sentenced to death, he escaped the agony of being hung, drawn and quartered by jumping from the scaffold and breaking his own neck.

WE HAVE THE LEFT OF WAY

6 Driving on the left is right, we all know that. This English 'rule of the road' dates to the times when your greatest danger on the highway was a sword attack, and it paid to be able to have your own sword arm (the right, for most people) near your potential foe. The ancient Greeks, Romans, Egyptians and even New York drove on the left until 1804. French trains still run on the left track, because we built most of them. Here, it was enshrined in a law ordering traffic to keep left on the crowded London Bridge, today in 1756. So basically, we're correct – right is wrong.

TIMES PAST

7 *The London Gazette* is one of the government's official journals of record, in which several statutory notices must be published. As such, it's not exactly a riveting read. But it has been published since today in 1665, making it the world's oldest surviving journal and worthy of our respect.

SHUSHING STUDENTS SINCE 1602

8 The Bodleian Library in Oxford is one of the oldest and largest libraries in Europe and was founded today in 1602 when Sir Thomas Bodley donated his books to furnish the nearly defunct university library. The 'Bod' was the first legal deposit library, and its many treasures include the Magna Carta, a Gutenberg Bible and Shakespeare's First Folio. It has 11 million items on 117 miles of shelving.

LET THERE BE LIGHT

9

Before this day in 1815, the naked flames of miners' lamps caused many tragic methane explosions. Then Cornish chemist Humphry Davy announced his invention of the safety lamp, which used a fine metal mesh to diffuse the flame's heat and prevent ignition of mine gases. Strangely enough, the widespread introduction of the 'Davy Lamp' actually increased accident figures, as mines previously considered too dangerous to work were reopened. Whoops. Still, Davy did also popularise the use of nitrous oxide (laughing gas), so at least he could smile about it all.

LOVERS OF FREEDOM

10

Today in 1960 was a turning point in English social history. *Lady Chatterley's Lover* by Nottinghamshire writer D.H. Lawrence finally went on sale after winning an obscenity trial that showed just how out of touch the stuffy 'Establishment' was with popular opinion. The prosecution famously asked if the novel were something 'you would even wish your wife or servants to read'. The jury could barely believe the pomposity, and promptly gave freedom of speech a much-needed boost. The book sold 3 million copies within 3 months. And it's a heck of a lot better written than *Fifty Shades of Grey*…

WE HAD IT FIRST

The famous yachting prize the America's Cup is the world's oldest international sporting trophy, but it isn't named after the country. It took the name of the schooner that won the challenge in 1851. The 'Auld Mug', as it is known to sea dogs, was originally the '£100 Cup', or 'Queen's Cup', of the Royal Yacht Squadron in Cowes. Much like America itself, we lost it and it's been theirs pretty much ever since. But we do still know a thing or two about boats – the Squadron (which took its name today in 1833) is the most prestigious yacht club in the world.

THE START OF RECORDED HISTORY

From the Beatles to Pink Floyd, Radiohead to Lady Gaga – the list of bands that have recorded at Abbey Road is a who's who of world music. EMI bought number 3 Abbey Road, St John's Wood, London, in 1929 and spent two years transforming it into the world's first custom-built recording studio. Today in 1931, Sir Edward Elgar conducted his famous recording of 'Land of Hope and Glory', played by the London Symphony Orchestra, in studio one, and Abbey Road was on its way to becoming the most famous recording studio in the world.

WORLD'S OLDEST BANGERS

13 The first London–Brighton car run was in 1896 when 54 cars (then new) went for a spin (named The Emancipation Run) to celebrate the raising of the speed limit and the scrapping of the escort with a red flag. But it was today's re-enactment in 1927 that put the eccentric event on the English calendar. Organisers insisted cars must be pre-1905, thereby establishing the London to Brighton Veteran Car Run, now the longest-running, and probably the slowest, motoring event in the world.

AND THIS WEEK'S NUMBER ONE IS ...

14 Before this day in 1952, the nation's top tunes were decided by sales of sheet music. Then Percy Dickens from the *New Musical Express* had the bright idea of asking shops for details of their record sales. He published the first pop chart – of 12 songs – which was topped by Al Martino with 'Here in My Heart'.

THE SHROPSHIRE OLYMPIAN

15 Today in 1850 Dr William Penny Brookes founded The Wenlock Olympian Society at Much Wenlock in Shropshire. This sporting festival (which continues to this day) gave gentlemen the chance to compete in games in the ancient Olympian tradition. Baron Pierre de Coubertin was so impressed when he visited the games in 1890 that he founded the International Olympic Committee and established the modern Olympic movement.

TREASURE BEYOND MEASURE

16 One of the world's most astonishing archaeological discoveries was made today in 1992 when Eric Lawes, a retired gardener and amateur metal detectorist, discovered the 'Hoxne Hoard'. Mr Lawes was looking for a farmer's lost hammer in a field in Sussex when he chanced upon 14,865 Roman coins and jewellery from the 4th century, totalling 7.7lb of gold and 52.4lb of silver. It is the largest such collection found anywhere within the Roman Empire. The British Museum paid Mr Lawes and the farmer £1.75 million for their historic discovery.

WE GOT THE WORLD TALKING

17

As any music fan could tell you, English is the world's favourite international language, its lovely tones travelling far and wide. This became official today in 1947, when the United Nations made English one of its two working languages (the other being French) and the one most often used. And, with 450 million English speakers worldwide, we have a head start in chatting people up on holiday. However, there are some words that don't travel so well – they are just too English. For example, there is one lovely word that you'll, regrettably, rarely hear outside of the country's borders:

BLIMEY

A TRADITIONAL CONTROVERSY ...

18 Hunting is a very divisive issue. Many country people support it; foxes don't. So you can either look on today's vote to ban the sport outright (MPs voted 321 to 204) in 2004 as the needless destruction of a noble and ancient English tradition by an interfering nanny state or the long-overdue abolition of a cruel, and pointless, practice. Either way, it's a notable day in our history. Particularly if you're a fox.

IDEAL LIVING

19 Our modern obsession with home-makeover shows on television like *Grand Designs* and *DIY SOS* can be traced back to this day in 1908 when the inaugural Ideal Home Exhibition opened at Olympia's grand hall in Kensington. The event was initially cooked up as a marketing stunt for the *Daily Mail*, which sponsored it for 100 years. It is now the biggest home show in the world.

'IT'S REAL PRETTY, BUT WHY THE HECK DID THEY BUILD IT SO CLOSE TO THE AIRPORT?'

20 For more than 1,000 years since William the Conqueror chose a nice safe hilly spot above the Thames, Windsor Castle has been home to English monarchs. This makes it the oldest inhabited castle in the world. It's also the largest: covering 13 acres, it is a fortification, a palace, and a small town. The castle acts as a major tourist attraction, a venue for state visits, and the Queen's favourite weekend bolthole. It was gutted by a devastating fire in 1992 that destroyed over 100 rooms – a fifth of the castle area. But today in 1997 it was reopened, fully restored to its former glory and ready for the next 1,000 years of English history.

HEAR HEAR, SEE SEE

21 Today in 1989, the first TV cameras were allowed into the House of Commons and the world could finally see how we do things in the crucible of democracy. Many MPs objected, fearing it could dumb down their debates. Because all that shouting, booing and flapping bits of paper at one other is so sophisticated, isn't it…

NOVEMBER

A TRUE HERO

22 Robin Hood is one of England's greatest heroes and, far from being just a myth, we know he existed – thanks to a book of accounts. The story goes that King Edward II went to Sherwood disguised as a monk to seek the famous outlaw. Robin robbed the supposed abbot, but had the decency to ask him to dinner. Over meat, he discovered Edward's identity and begged forgiveness. Edward was so charmed he took Robin into his service. But Robin soon grew weary of court. He pined so forlornly for Sherwood that the king let him return to his wild life. A fairytale? Well, an entry in King Edward's household expenses on this day in 1324 reads: 'To Robyn Hod, by command, owing to his being unable any longer to work, the sum of 5s.'

DOCTOR WHO

23 The nation's children first hid behind the sofa on this Saturday in 1963 as *Doctor Who* made its debut. The show's Daleks, Autons and Cybermen continued to terrify (and delight) kids for 26 years until the show was cancelled. The Doctor regenerated in 2005 and got back into the TARDIS for more classic time-travelling adventures. *Guinness World Records* credits Doctor Who as being the longest-running sci-fi show of all time.

ALL THE TIME YOU WANT, GENTLEMEN

24 Throughout most of its history, the Great English pub could open at all hours. As coaching inns they needed to be available for travellers. It was only with World War One's Defence of the Realm Act that licensing hours were restricted to encourage productivity. Finally, today in 2005, that outdated nonsense was done away with when 24-hour licensing was introduced. Once again we Englishmen and women could quaff our favourite tipple whenever we wanted. Which is quite a lot of the time, if we're being honest.

MUSICAL MILLIONS

25 On this day in 1984, Bob Geldof and 43 other members of Band Aid gathered in a London recording studio to sing 'Do They Know It's Christmas?'. They hoped it might raise £70,000 for famine-stricken Ethiopia; it became the biggest-selling single in UK chart history, shifting 3.5 million copies and raising millions of pounds. That was just the start of the positive impact that Band Aid had around the world. In 2005, the massive Live 8 concert in Hyde Park aimed to highlight the continuing struggle in Africa twenty years after the original Live Aid concert.

CSI LEICESTER

26

Today's hi-tech TV sleuths would be lost without Oxford-born geneticist Alec Jeffreys. In 1984 he was in his lab in the University of Leicester when he noticed distinct similarities and differences between the DNA of different members of a colleague's family. Almost instantly he realised the scope of his discovery – DNA fingerprinting, which uses variations in the genetic code to identify individuals. Within three years the first murderer had been convicted thanks to DNA profiling. Jeffrey's discovery put Leicester at the centre of forensic science and he was given the freedom of the city today in 1992, and knighted two years later.

STRIKE A LIGHT

27

Before today in 1826, making fire was fiddly and time-consuming. Then English chemist John Walker mixed up antimony sulphide, potassium chlorate and starch with gum and found it could be struck against any rough surface. He had invented the first friction match, which he called 'Congreves'. Walker refused to patent his revolutionary creation, either because he believed matches would be so beneficial to mankind that they should remain free to use, or because he thought his invention was too trivial. While he was dithering over this thorny philosophical point, his process was patented by a rival bright spark, Scottish-born inventor Sir Isaac Holden.

A BETTER CLASS OF SNACK

28 The Piccadilly super-pantry Fortnum & Mason is an English institution, but not just for Londoners too posh to go to Tesco. Today in 1738, the store invented that staple of our motorway service stations, the Scotch egg – over two centuries before Ginsters got anywhere near our English arteries. Back then Piccadilly was the Heston services of its day, full of coaching inns for travellers heading out of town, and a hand-sized meaty-egg snack was just the thing to pick up for the journey. F&M was also the first shop in England to take a chance on stocking Heinz baked beans – they were an expensive imported delicacy in the 1880s.

NELSON REACHES THE TOP

29 Vice-Admiral Horatio Nelson was one of England's greatest heroes. He worked his way up the ranks to become a captain aged just 20. He personally led boarding parties on enemy ships and won three of the greatest victories in our naval history at the Nile, Copenhagen and Trafalgar. Today in 1843 the stonework of the famous column honouring him in Trafalgar Square was finished. Contrary to myth, neither it nor the real Nelson wore an eye patch.

YOU'RE A SAUCY ONE

30 If anything goes perfectly with a proper English breakfast, it's HP Sauce. This tangy taste-enhancer was perfected today in 1895 by Frederick Garton, a Nottingham grocer. Garton chose 'HP' because he sold a batch to a restaurant in the Houses of Parliament. The original HP factory in Birmingham was later split by the A38(M), so they installed a pipeline that carried vinegar over the motorway.

DECEMBER

CLUELESS?

What could be more jolly than sneaking around the ballroom of a country house with your chums and some murder weapons, trying to work out who killed your host? Nothing, according to the millions of fans of Cluedo. The game was patented today in 1944 by Anthony E. Pratt, a solicitor's clerk from Birmingham, who wanted to give people something fun to do during air-raid drills. It was originally called simply 'Murder!'

ROUGH JUSTICE

Although England had long abolished capital punishment for murder, until today in 1997 it was still possible to be hanged for treason and piracy with violence. However, 2 December finally saw our statute books catch up with the mood of the nation and the punishment was changed to life imprisonment. And besides, there are not nearly half as many pirates around, or acts of treason for that matter, as there were when the laws first came into use – around the 1350s.

POTATO PIONEER

Europeans didn't have anything to go with their fish before today in 1586 – that's when Sir Thomas Harriot brought potatoes back to England from America. Harriot was a brilliant astronomer and mathematician who helped Sir Walter Raleigh navigate his way to and from the New World – and spot the potential of the mighty spud. He was also the first person to make a drawing of the moon through a telescope, which he did in July 1609, over four months before Galileo.

AMERICA HAS US TO THANK

4 Thanksgiving is one of the USA's biggest national celebrations, but it only exists thanks to 38 colonists from England. Today in 1619, they got out of their boat after landing in what is now the state of Virginia and promptly gave thanks to God for their safe arrival, an act that many believe started the Thanksgiving tradition.

GOING, GOING, STILL GOING ...

5 James Christie, founder of the famous auction house, brought the hammer down on his first sale today in 1766. He later capitalised on London's new status as the major centre of the international art trade following the French Revolution, building a reputation as the premier auctioneer of fine arts. Christie's has been based at King Street in St James's since 1823.

PAWS FOR THOUGHT

6 The only felines you see in most town parks are tabby cats harassing the pigeons. But in Forbury Gardens, Reading, you will find the world's largest lion. This 31-foot monster is the Maiwand Lion, unveiled today in 1886 to commemorate the loss of 286 local soldiers at the Battle of Maiwand in Afghanistan. The lion is one of the world's largest cast-iron statues. The soldiers' bravery became famous, and Sir Arthur Conan Doyle based Sherlock Holmes' sidekick Dr Watson on the regiment's medical officer.

IT'S PINING FOR THE FJORDS

7 Perhaps no other comedy show has had so many people quoting its lines the morning after as *Monty Python's Flying Circus*. The 'Beatles of comedy' weren't just fresh and funny, they were also hugely influential. Countless other comedy greats, from *The Simpsons* to Mike Myers and *South Park*, were inspired by their anarchic genius, and 'Pythonesque' has entered the English lexicon. Their surreal, silly and very English humour is typified by the 'Dead Parrot' sketch, from the show's first series, which was first broadcast today in 1969.

THE RAC GETS INTO GEAR

8

Inaugurated today in 1897, the Royal Automobile Club has done much to shape the motoring history of our country. In 1905, the Club organised the first Tourist Trophy (TT) motorcycle race, making that the world's oldest regularly run motor race. It also organised the first British Grand Prix in 1926. The Club introduced driving certificates in 1905, 30 years before the government decided to get involved. It also has one of the largest and most splendid clubhouses in London, on Pall Mall.

AY OOP, CHOOK!

9

Whether you're a fan or not, you have to admit that *Coronation Street* is an English institution. It first aired today in 1960, making it the world's longest-running TV soap opera currently in production. Few people thought it would run any sort of distance: it got mostly negative reviews and even its makers commissioned only 13 episodes. But viewers loved the believable characters and dramatic storylines. It was also groundbreaking – for many it was the first time they had heard Northern dialect such as 'nowt' and 'by heck!' at all, let alone on television.

NOBEL PRIZES AWARDED – TO US

10 England is the brainiest nation around – it's official. Today the prestigious Nobel prizes are awarded, and as of 2013 an incredible 75 of our brainboxes had received one. This is behind the USA's 305 brilliant boffins. But, when you consider that the Yanks have 307 million people and we only have 53 million, we clearly have a higher ratio of geniuses in our population.

WHAT DO GHOSTS EAT?

11 For over 160 years the bad joke, too-small paper hat and plastic toy that breaks in a millisecond have been an essential English Christmas tradition. All thanks to Tom Smith and his invention of the cracker, first sold today in 1847. He took the idea of the French bonbon (a sugared almond wrapped in a twist of tissue paper) and added a motto, toy and 'banging' strip to create his innovation – and earn himself a fortune in the process. His name still appears on the most famous brand of crackers. And it's 'spookghetti', by the way.

NORTH ATLANTIC OSCILLATION

12 It was in England that Guglielmo Marconi made his name as a pioneer of radio. He sent his first wireless transmission across the Atlantic Ocean today in 1901 at 12.30 p.m., from Poldhu in Cornwall to Newfoundland, Canada – 2,200 miles away. Often regarded as one of the key moments in science, this radio transmission contained just three clicks – or the Morse code signal for 'S'. Mind you, that could easily have been just a bit of static.

SAILING INTO HISTORY

13 Sir Francis Drake was every inch the national hero, repelling the Spanish Armada and becoming the first Englishman to circumnavigate the globe. He set out on this historic voyage today in 1577, returning three years later with his *Golden Hind* stuffed full of booty. Queen Elizabeth's half-share of this was more than the crown's other income for that entire year and she promptly knighted him. The Spanish, however, considered him a pirate. And they had a point: it was their treasure he had pinched.

LE PONT BRITANNIQUE

14

The Millau Viaduct (opened today in 2004) is the tallest bridge in the world, at 1,125 feet. It carries the A75–A71 autoroute over the River Tarn near Millau on its way from Paris to Montpellier. So why should we be proud of it? Well, this stunningly beautiful and technically amazing French masterpiece was designed by the eminent English architect Sir Norman Foster. Ooh la la.

HOOKER JOINS THE KEW

15

William Hooker from Norwich was a revolutionary botanist who developed the royal pleasure grounds at Kew into the world's foremost botanic gardens. Starting today in 1841, he expanded the gardens from 30 to 70 acres and the arboretum to 300 acres, had many new glass-houses erected and established a museum of economic botany. Kew has the world's largest collection of living plants (over 30,000); research here has helped the commercial cultivation of banana, coffee and tea, and has led to the production of many useful drugs, including quinine.

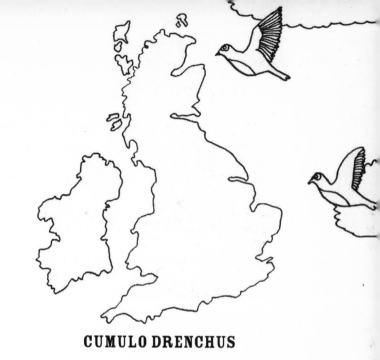

CUMULO DRENCHUS

16 We have enough of the blooming things, so it makes sense that an Englishman should name them – today in 1802, Luke Howard classified the different types of clouds. His basic terms were: *cumulus* (meaning 'heap'), *stratus* (meaning 'layer') and *cirrus* (meaning 'curl'), with various sub-categories. His bright idea of using Latin meant his terms transcended national boundaries, and meteorologists still use his system 200 years later. Howard also suggested that clouds form for a reason, and so founded the science of weather prediction. Which we're not so brilliant at.

DARTS GETS ROYAL APPROVAL

Pubgoers who enjoy a stint at the oche can pinpoint their hobby's worldwide popularity to this day in 1937. Darts had been enjoyed in one form or another for centuries: one theory states that it was first played by English archers throwing shortened arrows at the end of a fallen tree. But it was when King George VI and Queen Elizabeth played an impromptu game while visiting Slough Community Centre that the newspapers seized on the story and darts as a pastime really hit the bullseye. Whether their majesties also chinned 10 pints of lager and scoffed a few bags of pork scratchings has not gone down in history.

KING ARTHUR REAWAKENED

18 The story of King Arthur, with his knights of the round table, wizard-tutor Merlin and chivalric ideals, is one of the world's most popular myths. Arthur himself may have existed in the 6th century, but it was today in 1832 that large-scale interest in this legendary English king was reignited. Alfred, Lord Tennyson, published his famous poem 'The Lady of Shalott', firing the imagination of a Victorian society keen to espouse noble and heroic virtues.

WELCOME TO OUR WORLD

19 Born as the Empire Service in London today in 1932, the BBC's famous international broadcasting organisation became known as the World Service in 1965. It is now the world's largest international broadcaster, transmitting news and other programming in 32 languages to 188 million people every week.

THE BEST OF BRITISH BIKES

20 The Nottingham-based Raleigh Cycle Company was founded today in 1887 in the city's Raleigh Street. At first, it made just three bicycles a week, but grew rapidly to become the largest cycle manufacturer in the world, with over 10,000 employees and more than a million bikes sold per year by 1951. Competition came from cheaper cars and foreign cycle manufacturers, but there are still millions of us with happy memories of the first time we sped down the street on a supercool Chopper...

CAMELOT KING HEARD TO NOT LOSE

21 Until this day in 1913, sadistic wordsmiths had no way of inflicting tortuous misery on poor workers who simply wanted a nice puzzle to liven up their tea break. Then Arthur Wynne, an English journalist, published his 'word-cross' in the *New York World*. It was diamond-shaped and had no black squares and didn't quite grab the public's attention. But with a shape change, a switcheroo of the name and a few other tweaks, the modern crossword was born. And so the stage was set for millions of perfectly bright people to be baffled daily about whether clues about 'Underwater bananas travelling backwards to Cyprus, we hear' are meant to be anagrams or not.

THE SEWER KING

22 In the 1850s the River Thames was pretty much the world's largest open sewer. Raw waste also flowed in the streets, and 10,000 people would die from cholera in a year. Something had to be done. The Metropolitan Board of Works (founded today in 1855) handed the job to Joseph Bazalgette. His solution was to tear up every street in the city and lay a whole new system of waste piping. With admirable foresight, he realised this was something that could only be done once, so he massively over-engineered the project. Over 100 miles of huge trunk sewers were installed under new river embankments, as well as 1,000 miles of local pipes. And it did the trick: the river came back to life, cholera was wiped out and London had a model sewage system that still works today.

WE'VE GOT THE KNOWLEDGE

23 London cabbies sometimes get a bit of a rough ride, but 'The Knowledge', the rigorous test of London geographical lore that they must pass, is the world's most demanding training course for taxicab-drivers. Introduced today in 1865, it requires applicants to memorise 25,000 roads and 320 'runs' across town as well as all major places of interest. It usually takes two to four years of zooming round on a moped with an A–Z and 12 attempts at the exam to pass. Where to, Guv?

STUDENTS GRANTED

24 Cambridge routinely tops the world's best university lists and it dominates the Nobel Prize charts: 90 laureates have been associated with the university. Its first college was Peterhouse, which can trace its history back to this day in 1280, when Edward I allowed Hugo de Balsham to keep a Master and 14 'worthy but impoverished Fellows'. Students haven't changed much, then. As Oxford University had been founded a century or so earlier, this meant that England now had two universities; all the other countries in the world between them had one (the University of Bologna).

A STAR WATCHER IS BORN

25 Some scientists change the way we look at the world; Isaac Newton (born today in 1642) changed our perception of the entire universe. His revolutionary *Principia Mathematica* of 1687 sets out his three laws of motion, which form the basis of classical mechanics. It also includes his theory of universal gravitation, which was sparked when he (as legend has it) watched an apple falling from a tree in his orchard. You or I might have picked the apple up and eaten it – Newton spent the next twenty years calculating how the apple's descent related to the motion of cosmic bodies, thereby calculating gravity, the universal force that connects the vastness of space.

MORRIS DANCES BACK TO LIFE

26 Morris dancing has a history stretching back to the 15th century, but by the end of the 19th century this famous English tradition was almost extinct. Then today in 1899, folklore enthusiast Cecil Sharp saw a group of morris dancers performing at the village of Headington Quarry. He began collecting the dances and tunes, encouraging a morris revival. Today the tradition is thriving, with several hundred dance sides in the UK and more overseas. Which is great news for vendors of hankies.

THE INVENTION THAT REALLY CLEANED UP

27 What should one wipe with? The occupying Romans used sponges on sticks; rags and newspaper have also done the job. Lord Chesterfield kept a couple of pages torn from a volume of Horace in his pocket at all times – on sitting down, he would read the pages then use them. But the British Perforated Paper Company of Banner Street, London, was the first to really, ahem, take the matter in hand, when it launched its latest product today in 1880. Paper squares boxed fresh and ready – the first modern loo roll.

PEAK PERFORMANCE

28 Today in 1950 the Peak District became the country's first National Park, protecting 555 square miles of natural beauty and cultural heritage from damaging development. There are over 1,800 miles of public footpaths and long-distance trails in the Peak District, and with an estimated 22 million rucksacked and walking-booted visitors per year, it is thought to be the second most-visited national park in the world.

BIRDS FLYING HIGH

29

One English family has done more to help the world enjoy a quick pudding than any other – the Birds from Gloucestershire. Alfred Bird's wife was allergic to eggs but fancied something sweet, so the pharmacist whipped up a batch of egg-free custard today in 1837. She loved it so much he started selling it.

Today, Bird's Custard is so ubiquitous that most people don't know it's not true custard at all. Mrs Bird was also allergic to yeast, so Alfred promptly invented a new baking powder so she could enjoy bread. His son, Alfred Junior, did his bit by inventing egg powder, blancmange powder and jelly powder.

MIND THE GAP

30

Tower Bridge is one of this country's most famous icons, and today in 1952 it was the scene of a distinctively English bit of cool thinking. Bus driver Albert Gunter had just started over the bridge when it started to lift. Fearful of either sliding back or trundling into the Thames, Albert promptly slammed his foot to the floor and accelerated, whereupon he, the conductor, ten passengers and the double-decker all leaped the gap. Results: a broken spring for the bus and a £10 bonus to Albert for his quick thinking.

STRICTLY MEDICINAL

31 Today in 1600 the East India Company was granted a charter by Queen Elizabeth I of England. This organisation has something of a chequered history (at one point it imported more than 1,400 tons of opium a year into China) but, on the flipside, it did give the world the quintessentially English tipple – the gin and tonic. Realising that quinine helped prevent malaria, the company's officers consumed large quantities of tonic water, which is loaded with this beneficial drug. To improve the taste, it was of course necessary to also add medicinal quantities of gin. And ice, and lemon... Oh, and a sprig of mint.

Cheers to a splendid English year!

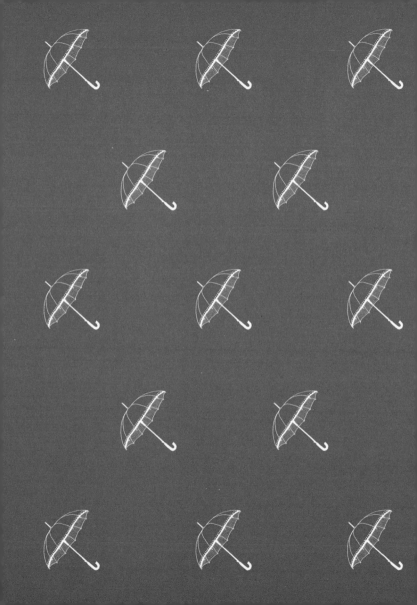